SHE CA...
DARKNE.........

She was soft and silent as Ruff pulled her to him beneath the blanket. Her hands were pleading as they tugged at his shirt.

"Is there some other way out for you?" he asked. "I hate to think of you chained for life."

She shook her head. "He is so old and I am so alone."

Ruff said nothing. His mouth tightened as he thought about Elena's situation, of the rich man waiting for her, of the end of her youth and happiness. Then he gave up worrying as Elena wriggled out of her dress with a demanding urgency. . . .

Wild Westerns by Warren T. Longtree

RUFF JUSTICE #11

COMANCHE PEAK

By
Warren T. Longtree

A SIGNET BOOK
NEW AMERICAN LIBRARY
TIMES MIRROR

PUBLISHED BY
THE NEW AMERICAN LIBRARY
OF CANADA LIMITED

PUBLISHER'S NOTE

This novel is a work of fiction. Names, characters, places, and incidents are either the product of the author's imagination or are used fictitiously, and any resemblance to actual persons, living or dead, events, or locales is entirely coincidental.

NAL BOOKS ARE AVAILABLE AT QUANTITY DISCOUNTS WHEN USED TO PROMOTE PRODUCTS OR SERVICES. FOR INFORMATION PLEASE WRITE TO PREMIUM MARKETING DIVISION, THE NEW AMERICAN LIBRARY, INC., 1633 BROADWAY, NEW YORK, NEW YORK 10019.

The first chapter of this book appeared in *Shoshone Run*, the tenth volume of this series.

First Printing, September, 1983

2 3 4 5 6 7 8 9

SIGNET TRADEMARK REG. U.S. PAT. OFF. AND FOREIGN COUNTRIES
REGISTERED TRADEMARK - MARCA REGISTRADA
HECHO EN WINNIPEG, CANADA

SIGNET, SIGNET CLASSIC, MENTOR, PLUME, MERIDIAN and NAL BOOKS are published in Canada by The New American Library of Canada, Limited, Scarborough, Ontario

PRINTED IN CANADA
COVER PRINTED IN U.S.A.

RUFF JUSTICE

He knew the West better than any man alive—a hostile, savage land rife with both violent outlaws and courageous adventurers. But Ruff Justice had a sixth sense that kept him breathing and saw his enemies dead. A scout for the U.S. Cavalry, he was paid to protect the public, and nobody was faster at sniffing out a killer, a crook, a con man—red or white, at close range or far. Anyone on the wrong side of the law would have to reckon with the menace of Ruff's murderously sharp stag-handled bowie knife, with his Colt pistol, and the Spencer rifle he cradled in his arms.

Ruff Justice, gentleman and frontier philosopher—good men respected him, bad men feared him, and women, good and bad, wanted him with all the wildness of the Old West.

1

·•••─◆─►────•••·

The tall man lay on his back on the bed, naked, warm, relaxed. The Colt hung in a shoulder holster hooked over the walnut headboard. Across the room Lorraine still stood at the window.

Ruff watched, fascinated. She had a way of striking sensuous poses unconsciously. Or maybe it wasn't all that unconscious.

"They're still there," Lorraine said in that husky baritone of hers, a voice meant for whispering love words. "Two of them. No, wait, there's another."

She bent over to peer out better. She had been watching the alley below them for ten minutes, fascinated by the men.

Ruff Justice yawned.

Lorraine was nude. She stood now with feet close together, her hips smooth and firm cocked toward Ruff as she bent over the sill, peering through the lace curtain of the hotel room. Her breasts, full and pendulous, swayed as she shifted position. Her hair, long, dark, and loose, fell across her golden shoulders. The line of her spine intrigued Ruff, running from the nape of her sleek neck across acres of smooth, delicately curved back to the hollow above her buttocks, where it was flanked by two dimples. There it tucked itself away between the two mounds of competent, challenging flesh. Ruff yawned and stretched again.

Lorraine turned toward the naked man on her bed, liking the sight of his hard, lean body against her lilac-colored sheet. "Aren't you going to do something?"

"If you'll give me the chance, woman," Justice said.

She smiled softly, with the satisfied, feline expression of a woman sated. It had been an hour since their intense afternoon of lovemaking had ended, but still Lorraine glowed with it.

"I meant about those men. Oh, Ruff, now they're even getting into your saddlebags!" She gave a little shriek and withdrew quickly from the window. "One of them looked up at me. Right at me."

"Stay away from the window, then," Justice said, lazily rolling to his side, propping himself up on one arm to look at Lorraine. "Come over here." He patted the bed.

"But they're down there," she said breathlessly. "What do they want? Who are they?"

"Can't you forget about them?"

"They frighten me, Ruff. I'm not used to having men watch my windows."

That, Ruff decided, wasn't necessarily true. Or the men of Corbett City just weren't imaginative. Justice would have spent a good deal of time watching her window, given the chance. She came to him, kneeling down on the floor beside the bed so that her full, pink-nippled breasts rested on the mattress. Lorraine had the body a sculptor only dreams of. It was hearty, eager, firm, and nearly intimidating. It was a challenge to mortal man. But then Ruff Justice had always enjoyed a challenge.

He leaned over, grazed her breasts with his lips, and felt her hand rest on his head.

"Make them go away," she said.

Justice sighed, sitting up. He nodded, swung his feet to the floor, and sat for a minute. Lorraine placed her hands on his thighs and smiled up at him, producing a counterproductive reaction.

"They're really not bothering anything," Justice said.

"It gives me the shivers knowing they're out there. Doesn't it disturb you?"

"I've gotten used to them." They'd been clomping around after Justice for three days now, clumsily stalking him, half-hiding themselves in shadows as he walked past, tiptoeing after him in heavy cowboy boots, eyeing him from behind newspapers. They weren't much good at their job, but they were dedicated.

"What do they want?" Lorraine asked. "Why are they following you?" Who, in fact, was the tall man she had been entertaining for the last week? A lawman, an outlaw? She knew nothing about him except that he was tall, lean, hard. That he wore his dark, gently waving hair long, that his dark mustache drooped to his jawline. That he was never without a weapon at hand. That he was both expert and enthusiastic as a lover. That he called himself Ruff Justice.

Now he rose and padded across the room, yawning as he went. He sat on Lorraine's delicate, padded dressing chair and put on his ruffled white shirt. Standing, he stepped into his dark trousers. Tugging up his shiny black boots, dropping his cuffs over them, he returned to the bed, taking the pocket holster and Colt .41 from the headboard. Lorraine had eased up onto the bed and she now sat cross-legged on the bed, hands tucked under her long, tapered thighs, watching.

Justice walked to the mirror, strapping on the holster. He tied his dark tie, leaned forward to peer at his face, brushed back his long hair with Lorraine's dressing-table hairbrush, winked at her in the mirror, and turned to put on coat and hat.

"You won't be long?"

"Not long at all," he promised, kissing her.

"But you won't get hurt?"

"No," he answered, since that was the answer she wanted and expected. He couldn't very well tell her that if she looked out the window she might see him shot to pieces. He didn't intend on being hurt; but then he never had, and he had been hurt despite intentions many times, sometimes seriously. And one day it would be worse than that. "No," he repeated anyway, "I won't get hurt."

"Hurry back?" She threw strong arms around Ruff as he bent over her, and hugged him to her substantial breast.

"Right back," he said. He was beginning to wonder about the quality of Lorraine's mind, but then it wasn't exactly her intellectual prowess that had drawn Ruff to her. Stimulating conversation was all very well—before dark—but hardly necessary. She hugged him again enthusiastically and Ruff thought he heard his spine crack.

"Rest," he told her, "you'll need it." Then he crossed the room to the door and went out, locking it.

The hallway was dark, narrow, and silent. A single oil lamp burned at the elbow of the corridor. Somewhere a woman raised her voice briefly in an accusing tone and then was silent.

Ruff moved to the end of the corridor and looked left and then right. To the left the stairs descended into the hotel lobby and front door. To his right was only a window, tall and narrow.

Pressing his face to the glass, Ruff could see a sloping ledge and the alley below. He unlatched the window and yanked hard. He doubted it had been opened since the hotel was built, but finally it came free of its encrustation of dried paint and putty, and slid open.

Justice stepped out onto the ledge, closing the window behind him. He crouched, peering up and down the alley. From farther uptown he heard the shout of a man, the high-pitched laughter of a woman, followed by the tinkling of glass. Somewhere a piano played loudly, the musician working around a broken string as he picked out "Dixie."

Justice walked along the shingled, sloping ledge, rounding the corner of the hotel until he was within sight of his white-faced gray horse.

The horse stood patiently at the hitch rail behind the hotel's rear entrance. On the ground beside it the contents of Ruff's saddlebags were scattered. Across the alley was the back of the Meadows Stable and adjoining corral. Directly below Ruff Justice was a crouched, bearded man with a rifle in his hands.

Ruff set himself and jumped silently from the ledge, landing with a jolt, his boots square against the waiting gunman's back. The man went down and out without so much as a sigh. Ruff picked up the rifle and flung it into the darkness behind him.

He crouched, stripping off the gunman's heavy buffalo coat, which he slipped on over his suit. The smell of it reminded him to ask Lorraine where he could get his laundry done.

Rising, Ruff proceeded unhurriedly up the alley. Looking to his right as he passed the stable, he noticed three saddled horses standing at the far end of the building. Ruff himself kept to the deep shadows next to the building, pausing before the wide-open double doors.

"Lou?" a whispery voice called.

"Huh?"

"Where's Jake?"

Ruff didn't answer this time. Snarling a curse, the other man slipped away. Ruff waited, looking around, smelling the rank buffalo coat, wondering if the stink of it would stick to his suit.

Then he entered the stable, looked through toward the interior court, where the three horses waited. The gunmen would eventually have to pass through here again. Ruff decided to hurry the process along.

Searching the walls of the stable, he found a roll of baling wire among the tools. Whistling, he walked between the two rows of stalls and crouched down beside a twelve-by-twelve upright, wrapping one end of the wire around the timber at a point a foot from the ground. The other end was similarly secured around a post opposite. Justice returned the wire to its hook before he walked back, stepping over the strung wire, and went to the open door of the stable.

There again was the gunman who had called to him.

"Where in hell's Jake?"

"I don't know," Ruff whispered, "I'm Justice." Then he turned and ran through the stable. It was a second before the stunned thug reacted and ran after him. Justice actually had to slow down as he ran through the stable, leaped the wire, and continued toward the saddled horses.

In a moment, however, he heard a whistle, the thudding of running, booted feet, and the gunman appeared. Justice took to his heels again, racing into the interior courtyard. He heard the clomping boots and a sudden thud. He sighed and walked back into the stable.

The gunman lay sprawled on the ground, out cold. His head had whacked against the upright as he tripped on the wire. Justice took his guns and flung them into the loft.

While at that, he spotted the block and tackle overhead. Finding the tieline, he lowered the hay hook, which was suspended from the tackle, hooked it through the outlaw's belt, stuffed the man's own scarf into his mouth, tied his hands behind his back with his own belt, and ran him up to hang in midair, peacefully asleep.

Ruff yawned, scratched his arm, wondered if there were little animals in the buffalo coat, and went back into the alley. He peered into the big rain barrel that sat near the door, saw there were only a few inches of water in it, and tipped it out carefully, not wanting to spot his newly polished town boots.

Uprighting it, he looked around the deserted alley. In another moment it wasn't empty. He spotted a man trying to catfoot it past Ruff's horse. The gray looked at him in a detached manner.

Ruff yawned again—he had to get more sleep—lifted a long leg up and over, and stepped into the rain barrel. From there he called out.

"Jake!"

"Huh!"

Ruff winced at the dull sound of Jake's voice. Why couldn't people hire better help?

"Up here," Justice said, putting a snarl in his tone.

Jake came a-running. Ruff heard the pounding of his feet, then the slower squish of boots over the muddy ground where he had dumped out the rain barrel.

"Where are ya?" Jake called out.

Justice rose from the barrel, brought down the butt of his Colt against Jake's skull, and watched the man fold up, slumping to the alley.

Ruff stepped from the rain barrel, discarded the buffalo coat, and dragged Jake inside the stable. Lowering the hay hook again, he tied Jake and then ran him up to dangle beside his partner.

Then, straightening his tie and hat, Justice walked back toward the hotel room. He had better things to do.

2

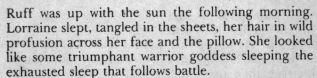

Ruff was up with the sun the following morning. Lorraine slept, tangled in the sheets, her hair in wild profusion across her face and the pillow. She looked like some triumphant warrior goddess sleeping the exhausted sleep that follows battle.

Justice picked his dark suit up from the chair and hung it on a closet hanger. From the closet he took his beaded buckskins. He sat on the chair, rested his head on a hand for a long minute, watching the patch of sunlight creep across the hardwood floor toward his bare foot.

He looked again at the bed. It was inviting, but Justice had already squeezed his schedule too tightly. Sighing, he rose and pulled on his buckskin pants. His soft fringed boots were next. He checked the little skinning knife in its boot sheath, and stood and walked to the mirror, looking at his lean, somewhat mournful face.

Digging out his shaving soap and brush, he lathered up and scraped away at the dark beard, carefully avoiding the long dark mustache, which now hung to his jawline.

That finished, Justice pulled his beaded shirt on over his head. Using Lorraine's brush, he swept the tangles out of his dark hair.

Ruff crossed to the window and stood looking out at Corbett City. The town was coming to life now. Storekeepers swept off their section of boardwalk. The blacksmith's hammer was already ringing down the street. A couple of barefoot kids and their spotted dog were racing somewhere.

Justice saw no one lingering in the alley, and he figured Jake and his friends had had enough. He hoped so. He didn't want to go on fighting them all the way to Mexico. They had guns, and no matter how unskilled a man is, he's dangerous once he has a gun in his hand.

Justice had put away the little .41 he carried in town. Now he unrolled his hip holster and strapped it on. He drew the long-barreled .44 Colt and swung the cylinder out, checking the action and his loads. In the corner stood his .56 Spencer repeater. He supposed it was getting old-fashioned now, that rifle of his. Seven-shot magazine as opposed to the seventeen rounds a fully loaded Henry "needle gun" could carry; but Justice was used to it, and there had been damn few times, even in Indian country, when seven shots hadn't done the job. Besides, he liked that .56 bullet. There was enough shocking power to make sure that what he hit went down. It shot long and flat, it was accurate and comfortable. Now he checked out the Spencer too. Satisfied, he shouldered it, holding the barrel.

Then he looked back at the bed. He wouldn't kiss her good-bye. One kiss led to another. He simply picked up his saddlebags and went out, leaving Lorraine to her tangled dreams.

His horse's ears went up eagerly as it spied Ruff. He walked to the leggy, white-faced gray and patted its neck. Saddling, he rode it to the general store, where he picked up a sackful of supplies, including —to the storekeeper's puzzlement—pen and ink and a ledger book. Ruff also purchased tinned beef/ and a side of bacon. Rice, beans, and four cans of pears completed his shopping list. He already had two hundred rounds of ammunition in his saddlebags.

"Traveling far?" the storekeeper asked.

"Saltillo."

"In Mexico?" The man looked up, squinting at Ruff through his spectacles.

"That's right."

"I thought that was where they were having all that trouble with this fellow Chato Chavez and that private army of his."

"That's what they tell me." Ruff shouldered his sack of goods and turned toward the door.

"Well, watch yourself, friend."

That was what Ruff intended to do, although there was no guarantee that watching would be enough. Not with Chavez. Not with Kyle Dunweather.

It was Dunweather who had put the inefficient thugs on Ruff's trail. Dunweather who would be back to try to stop Ruff Justice again. He had a lot to lose. If Ruff was lucky, he might make this journey without running into Chavez. It was said the Federales had him running toward the Sierra Madre. But he would certainly see Dunweather again. That accounted for the extra ammunition Justice was carrying.

The gray walked slowly southward and Justice let his horse pick its own pace. The land was raw and empty. Red sand, red buttes, red mesas. On the flats there were slender threads of green along the washes where some water still ran in pencil-thin silver courses. Dry, very dry, Ruff thought. It would be a tough run up for Trujillo.

Ruff turned in his saddle and looked back across the empty land, seeing nobody. But they would be coming sooner or later.

It had started with Kyle Dunweather's greed.

Dunweather had been the beef supplier for Fort Sumner and several other small New Mexico Territory outposts. This was dry country most times and there were few available sources of army beef. Dunweather, close in to Fort Sumner on the Pecos River, had been a natural choice.

A tall, dry, surly man with a wisp of red beard, Dunweather was a displaced Texan. He had moved his whole outfit after the war, driving his herd west. He had a fierce hatred of carpetbag law, the Yankee army, as he called it, Indians, Mexicans, and of just about anything else he did not own. He was feudal, demanding fierce loyalty from his men, who were for the most part ex-Confederate soldiers, fighting men to the bone.

He was also greedy.

He had sold the army short, delivered short beef supplies to the reservation Indians, and finally unloaded a herd of infected animals on a bribed or incompetent quartermaster.

"I won't deal with the man," Colonel Hollingshead had said angrily.

"Sir," Lieutenant York had argued, "there is no other choice. The men are living off of game and flour now. The reservation Indians cannot do the same. Not unless we allow them off of the agency, armed—and that would raise a political stink detectable in Washington."

"No," Hollingshead said, "you're right there. Our people haven't been tame that long. I ride through that reservation and I recognize half of those people. Manto's Chiricahua's, Long Nose's Comanches. I don't have the confidence to let them off the agency. Besides, the settlers would raise pure hell, as you suggest. But if we can't feed them, York, we've got an even more potent situation brewing."

"Then use Dunweather."

"No. Dammit, I won't. The man's a bandit." He turned toward the other man in the room. The man in buckskins who sat in a wooden chair, legs crossed at the knees, wide-brimmed white hat on his lap. "You haven't said anything, Justice."

"No." Ruff rubbed his jaw thoughtfully. "I do have a suggestion, but I'm afraid it won't go down too well either."

Hollingshead frowned at Justice and then shrugged.

"If you've got a suggestion to make, Justice, throw it in the pot. What's on your mind?"

"Mexican beef."

"What?" Hollingshead had begun trimming a cigar with his penknife. Now he halted, his frown deepening. "Did you say Mexican beef?"

"I did."

"From where?" Hollingshead asked, his eyes narrowing. All the while he was considering the political stink something like that would cause. Dunweather would scream his head off.

"Saltillo." Justice recrossed his legs. "I've a friend down there, sir. His name's Carlos Trujillo, but he was born an American."

"Then how . . .?"

"His mother was Mexican. When Trujillo's father was killed at Chancellorsville during the war, his mother pulled up stakes and returned to her family. Carlos has been there ever since. He inherited the family rancho when his mother died, and he's run it since then."

"Can't do it," Hollingshead said. Then again, "Can't do that."

"All right," Justice replied.

"How many beef has he got?"

"I don't know exactly, but his place is one of those old grants—close on to a quarter of a million acres."

"I see." Hollingshead thoughtfully lit his cigar.

"Still, sir, there is no precedent for this, and it could be quite dangerous," Lieutenant York put in.

"Politically," Hollingshead said.

"Yes, sir."

"Could be a lot more dangerous if those reservation Indians decide to break out," Justice pointed out. "And I don't mean politically. I know you gentlemen have to worry about careers and all, but you've got a flesh-and-blood situation on your hands."

"Things are pretty unsettled down that way, aren't

they?" Colonel Hollingshead asked, his thoughts returning to Mexico.

"Chavez?"

"Exactly." The bandit had managed to gather himself what amounted to an army. More than one pueblo had been burned to the ground. The man saw himself as a Napoleonic figure, leading his people out of the life of hardship they now endured. Of course, if a few of them had to be killed in order to make their lives happier, that was just too damned bad.

"They say he's headed west and south, sir."

Hollingshead stood rocking on his heels, his cigar clamped between his teeth. He didn't have any good options here, and he knew it.

York was staring helplessly at his commanding officer, afraid of what was going on in his mind.

"I guess that's all for now," Hollingshead said abruptly. "I'll give it some consideration."

York flushed with relief and saluted. Turning on his heel, he went out the door.

Justice had begun to follow him, but the colonel said, "Wait a minute, will you, Justice?"

He then walked to the door, glanced out into the orderly room, and shut it.

"The boy's young and ambitious, Justice," the colonel said. "He knows how this will go down up above."

"You want the Mexican beef."

"Damn right I do. But the way we have to do it doesn't follow the army book. If I write up a requisition and send it through channels, it will be denied. Even if it were approved, it would be too late. We need that beef, and we need it as soon as we can get it."

"You're putting your neck on the block," Justice said.

"Yes." The colonel nodded. "But as you pointed out, it's my head or the head of a lot of innocent people. At least that's what I fear." He turned to look out the window at the soldiers drilling on the parade ground. "Hell, I'll never see a brigadier's star anyway, Justice. They can push me out the door, I suppose, but that's about all."

"You'll want me to handle this?"

"You'll have to. Alone, I'm afraid. I obviously can't send any soldiers into Mexico. As for the money"—the colonel stifled a grin—"I suppose I'll have to finagle that while you're gone."

"You're showing a real talent for this, sir," Justice said.

"Maybe I should have gone into quartermaster myself." The colonel's mood changed abruptly. "It's not going to be any fun for you, Ruff. If Dunweather gets onto this, he'll try and stop you one way or the other."

"I realize that, sir."

"If there was another way . . . But there isn't, Justice. There's no other damned way. I'm going to feed my people and I'm going to feed my Indians."

Assuming Ruff got through. That went unspoken. That afternoon Justice had saddled up and ridden out. At Corbett City he had wired Trujillo and settled in to wait. The answer had been a long while coming, but it had been affirmative.

Now Justice looked around him and measured the land by eye. His reckoning was that he was now into Mexico, into Chavez's land. And on his backtrail were a few no-accounts Dunweather had hired to plant his belly full of lead—or his back.

Still, Justice was pleased to be out here. It was still cool this time of the year and the desert was long and clean, with here and there inexplicable clusters of yellow wild flowers. He had a good horse under him and a good rifle in his hand. It was all he had asked for on many occasions.

He tugged his hat lower and followed the ribbon of a creek into the southern lands.

He camped that night in the cedar-stippled hills that had begun to rise out of the flatlands. There was much sage and some manzanita. And plenty of cholla cactus.

He made no fire, but sat near his hobbled horse, watching the desert flush to a deep red and then go crimson before night put out the candle.

With the dawn he was up again and riding.

It would be good to see Carl again—or Carlos. He had been a slender, reticent kid when Justice had known him. Out of Tubec, Ruff had needed a translator badly. This reedy boy with the rifle slung carelessly in the crook of his arm had stepped up and volunteered. It had saved a deal of bloodshed. Carlos had stayed on with the army for a month or two and Justice had gotten to know him fairly well. It was then he had heard Carlos Trujillo's story.

Ruff had been with him when Carlos had gotten the letter telling him his mother had died. He had watched the kid, hunched over with grief, ride off to the south. It would be good to see him again in these better times.

For some time Justice had been paralleling a set of tracks. Now, he noticed another horseman had joined the first. He noted this with only a vague corner of his mind. There was nothing strange about two riders deciding to continue together, nothing strange about them following the same route Ruff himself was using. It was where the creek ran, and without water a man didn't travel far in this country.

Toward sundown, when Justice was looking for a place to camp, he noticed the wisp of smoke rising farther ahead. Simultaneously he noticed that there were now four horsemen in the group traveling ahead of him.

Justice frowned and glanced westward. Where had they come from? There was nothing much that way but the broken hills, the vast desert.

Instinctively Ruff guided his horse away from the creek, heading eastward. Caution had kept him alive longer than some he could name, and he felt uneasy about this bunch.

His camp was up a shallow canyon where nothing but greasewood grew, where the land was dry and hard, great dark stony outcroppings pushing out from the walls of the gorge.

He camped without fire again, eating a tin of pears, a· tin of beef, washing it down with canteen water. Then, with his Colt still strapped on, Justice rolled up in his blanket to sleep while the desert night went chill and the huge diamond stars blinked on one by one.

He awoke hours later in the cold of the canyon night, his eyes fluttering open, his body rigid, his heart hammering in his chest.

He lay there knowing something was wrong, not knowing what it was. His eyes moved. Only his eyes. Shifting from side to side as his thumb found the hammer of his Colt.

The gray was standing to his right, ears pricked curiously. The stars were huge and close in the inky sky. Still Justice did not move, although his deeper instincts told him that something was wrong.

In another second he was glad he had not moved. A star was there and then it was not. Something had come between Justice and the thin starlight, blocking it off. In another moment he made out the shape of a hat, the dark bulk of shoulders.

Still Justice did not move. He looked to the left, his hand tightening on the grip of his revolver. He heard the whisper of boot leather over sand and saw the second man. And a third.

"That's close enough," Justice said in a taut whisper. He saw the man to his right jerk upright.

"There are four of us, *hombre*," a dry voice answered.

"Leave now and there'll be four of you still," Justice said.

There was a moment's hesitation and then the voice responded. "*Amigo*, you stay put, eh? We just want to see what you have in your saddlebags. Nothing worth dying for, eh?"

"That's for you to decide," Justice said, his voice even, soft.

"Kill him," the man on Ruff's left said, and the night exploded with the thunder of the guns.

To Justice's left a gun stabbed flame, the report deafening. But Justice was already moving; firing once through his blanket, he rolled to his right, coming to a knee.

A man screamed out with pain as Justice's first shot tagged flesh and bone. He was hurled back before the impact of the .44 slug, to lie moaning against the earth. Justice barely heard him. The roar of the guns blotted out all other sound.

Justice felt a near bullet whiff past his ear and he triggered off, aiming for the black, star-silhouetted figure to his right. He saw the man's hands thrown up wildly, saw him start to topple. Then Justice was already switching his sights. A man lunged at him out of the darkness and the big .44 spoke again, its terrible thunder splitting the night. A body hit him hard, a heavy, sweat-scented body. Justice grappled with it, but there was no need.

The body lay across Ruff's leg, soaking in warm blood. There were three dead, and Justice saw the last man racing down the canyon. In another moment he heard the horse, saw the rider, bent low across the withers, flagging the pony with his hat as he rode hell for it down the canyon.

Ruff lifted his pistol, changed his mind, and lowered it again. He sat there for a minute, the weight of the dead robber on his legs. He shoved fresh loads into his pistol, ejecting the warm, dead casings.

Then, kicking the dead man aside, he rose, wiping back his long dark hair. He moved cautiously across the camp, eyes still alert, searching.

"You're a big help," he told the white-faced gray horse, which looked at him with wide, starlit eyes.

"You're supposed to let me know if anyone's prowling, you jackass."

The gray bowed its head as if in shame, and Ruff laughed, stroking the animal's neck. Then he found his blanket and saddle and rigged up.

Number Four might be coming back. He might have some friends. Justice was tightening his cinch when he heard the low groan. Turning, he saw the man move. His hands scrabbled at the earth. In the starlight his eyes were white, ghostly as he looked up at Ruff Justice.

"*Señor, por favor . . .*"

Justice walked beside him and crouched down. He was a kid of eighteen or so, lying there soaked in his own blood on this chill night up this desolate canyon. That's what happens, Justice thought, when you decide the other man's got no rights. When you puff up and go out, gun in hand, to rob somebody.

The sensible thing to do was to put another bullet through his head.

Justice gritted his teeth and opened up the kid's shirt, first searching him for a hideout gun or a knife.

"I am dying," the kid moaned.

"Likely."

"You shot me."

Justice didn't answer.

"That hurts!" he screamed as Ruff touched the tender area around the wound. It should have hurt. The bullet had plowed in beneath the collarbone on the right side, the slug shredding meat, shattering bone, the energy of the slug sledgehammering the organism. That shock is a terrible thing, something someone who has never been tagged can't understand. It's like being hit by a freight train when a heavy-caliber bullet meets flesh.

Justice flicked a match alight with his thumbnail, squinting at the kid's damaged shoulder as the flame bent and twisted in the night breeze.

"Don't let me die!" The kid gripped Ruff's arms. His head came up, the tendons on his neck standing taut, his face twisted into a terrible grimace.

"Lie back," Justice growled. "Save your energy."

Cursing himself for a fool, Justice got to work on the wound, cleaning it as best he could, sprinkling flour over it to help the coagulation. All the time he was looking across his shoulder, listening for the sounds of approaching hoofbeats. Number Four had gotten away; maybe Number Four was on his way back now with Numbers Six and Seven, Twenty-eight . . .

"Sit up now. Hold your arm like this. That hurt? I'm going to strap it against you. That's the best I can do."

"I can't stay here!"

"Maybe your friend will come back for you."

"I will die."

Then Ruff thought the kid had died. He fell back suddenly, his mouth gaping, his eyes closing slowly. Ruff felt for and found a pulse. The kid had just gone out from the lack of blood.

Justice finished strapping up the arm, trying to keep it immobilized. There was broken bone in that shoulder, obviously, and it had to be kept from moving around.

That completed, Ruff sat back on his heels, looking down the canyon. There he sat, like the fool of all time, worried about the little bastard who had come to murder him for the few trifles in his saddlebag.

And now? To go off and leave the kid was a sentence of death. A bullet would be more merciful. There was nothing to do but tote him along, try to find a doctor or at least a house where he could be put to bed. If he made it that far—and right now that didn't look promising.

Justice searched around and found the little pinto pony down the canyon tied loosely to a clump of

brush. He led the horse back up the canyon, still
shaking his head in wonder at his own folly.

The kid had to be thrown over the horse's back;
there was no other way. Ruff tied his hands to one
stirrup, his feet to the other. Then, stepping into
leather himself, he led on out of the gorge, looking
behind him to where the badly wounded outlaw
jounced along on the pinto's back—and ahead to the
empty, dark desert where other men waited, men
who would have no compunctions about leaving Ruff
Justice to die against the cold, hard earth.

3

Dawn was a harsh red glare in the eastern skies, an endless sweep of red desert, a weary gray horse between Ruff Justice's legs. Crimson-tipped ocotillo thrust tentaclelike, thorny whips against the sky. The horse's long, wavering shadow floated darkly across the sand.

In an hour it was warm on the desert, and there was no water. Justice had stayed well away from the creek road. It was noon when he stopped, lifted the kid's head, and found he was still alive. He untied him and took him down from the horse's back, laying him in the thin shade of a mesquite bush. Justice stood for a moment, hands on hips, looking down into the deathly pallid face of the Mexican. Then, shaking his head, he knelt down, opening his canteen.

"Here. Drink this," he growled. The kid didn't stir and Ruff shook him.

"Magdalena . . ." the boy groaned.

"No. She's not here. Drink this."

The kid suddenly came alert enough to realize that it was water he was being offered, that his throat felt fiery, his body parched, and he made a grab for Ruff's canteen, spilling it over his face.

"Easy, vaquero."

The kid drank, choking on the water, his eyes studying with fright and amazement the tall man crouched over him. Justice pulled the canteen away before the kid was through.

"You know of a town near here?" Justice demanded.

The kid didn't answer and Justice shook him sharply. "Where is a town? A doctor? You're going to die if I don't get you some help."

"No town, no town," the kid answered through cracked lips.

"You a wanted man?" Justice asked.

"Yes. Wanted."

"There's no help for it. You can go to jail or die here. It's up to you."

"They will hang me, *señor*."

Hang or die on the desert, that was the kid's choice, was it? Tough. Ruff was having trouble dredging up a lot of sympathy for the kid. If they wanted to hang him, he had been involved in something before. He had been perfectly willing to see Justice die.

The trouble was, dammit, Ruff wasn't willing to let the kid kick off.

"All right," Justice said, standing. "Is there any place you can go?"

"Maybe." His eyes brightened. "The Zopilote. It is not far. South, maybe ten miles."

"Zopilote. What's that?"

"A cantina, only a cantina and some shacks. A place where—"

"An outlaw hideout."

"*Sí*. That is it."

"Uh-uh. Can't take you there, friend. I don't like the people you know."

"It is the only place. María can heal me. She is *india*. She knows the herbs."

"I said no!" Ride into an outlaw hideout to deliver a man who had tried to kill him. Not likely. Besides, he was wasting valuable time. The Trujillo ranch was a long way off and Justice didn't have much time to get down there and bring that herd back up.

"There is no other place. You may as well let me die." The kid lay back again, his dark eyes closing, his pale face streaked with dirt, smudged with blood, his upper lip curled back over even white teeth. He trembled with agony.

Justice turned away from him angrily. He stood looking out across the desert. Saltillo was east from where he now stood. Zopilote—"buzzard"—to the south. There were men out there who would cut his throat for a peso. And one wounded kid who was going to die if he didn't get some help.

Justice walked back to the young outlaw, and after looking at him for a minute, he picked him up too roughly and carried him to his horse.

"Where . . .?"

"Zopilote," Ruff Justice said between his teeth.

The kid didn't respond. He couldn't. He had passed out again, with a faint smile still playing on his lips.

Justice rode through the heat of the day, his eyes red and gritty, his body sweaty, prickly. The collar of his shirt chafed at his neck. The sun glared off the sands. From time to time he got down to check the kid, half-hoping he had gone, but the outlaw was tenacious: he clung to life. Justice led him southward, toward someone called María in some place called Zopilote, somewhere in Mexico.

He came upon the town at dusk. Zopilote was squat, small, and dilapidated. The cantina, the largest building, was of adobe plastered white. The walls glowed a dull violet in the dusky light. Around it was a collection of small shacks, a pole corral, and back up among the oaks behind the cantina another structure that might have been a smithy—Ruff could just make out an iron pipe rising from the sod roof.

Justice stepped down from the gray, walking back to the pinto. The kid was alive. Barely. His pulse was light and fluttery. Justice settled in to wait until dark.

Three men rode into town from the south as Justice watched. They dismounted in front of the cantina and clomped in across the wooden porch. Half an hour later another man came in from the north. When it was full dark, Justice led off down the

gulley to the west, circling Zopilote, making toward
the oaks. From the cantina he heard the distinctive
sounds of a guitar, and once the shout of a man. No
one else was on the streets; no one else seemed to
live in this godforsaken hole.

It was dark and cool beneath the oaks. Ruff led
the horse up to the building there. He looked inside,
his Colt in hand, discovering that he had been right.
It was a smithy, but the forge was cold. There were
spiderwebs strung across the doorway. It was empty
and apparently long unused.

Justice untied the kid, dragged him from the horse,
and placed him on the ground. Then he walked to
the verge of the trees, peering out of the shadows
toward the back of the cantina.

Someone came out of the back door, and Justice
froze. He couldn't be seen in that light, his body
merging with the trunks of the trees, or so he hoped.

He watched silently as the figure moved across the
yard toward what appeared to be a chicken coop.
Then he moved. Crouched low, he filtered through
the shadows, his eyes flickering.

It was a woman he had seen. Of middle years with
a full but not fat figure. Dressed in a dark skirt and
white blouse, she was, he hoped, María. How many
women could be living and working in this cross-
roads to nowhere?

Ruff was beside the coop, smelling the old wood,
the chicken droppings. He heard a woman cooing to
a chicken. Then the startled squawk as a hand closed
around its neck.

There was a soft chuckle from the woman and
then utter silence.

"Who is there?" she asked.

"María?"

"Yes."

"There is a man wounded. He is asking for you."

There was another long silence and then a round
face, wide eyes, peering around the corner of the

coop. She held the chicken, its neck wrung, in her strong brown hand.

"Who are you?"

"You don't know me, but someone you do know is hurt back there. Up by the smithy."

María looked back fearfully at the cantina. "Is a lie?" she asked.

"Come and see. There's little time."

She nodded firmly. "All right. I trust you this one minute."

Ruff smiled, pointing up the hill. "Come on."

She fell in behind him, chicken still in hand. They entered the oaks silently and in another minute they were beside the wounded man.

"Alfredo!" Maria gasped, going to her knees.

"You know him?"

"Yes, yes, yes. Alfredo! I knew it. One day I knew this would happen. To run with men like you leads to this," she said, turning snarling on Justice. "What happened?"

"He tried to rob somebody."

María nodded. She was undoing Ruff's bandaging, examining the shoulder. Her mouth turned down in a terrible frown. "Bad, bad," she hissed.

"You will take care of him?"

She turned amazed eyes on Ruff. "Of course. You will help me carry him to the cantina."

"No."

"No!" she exploded. "Not even that for your *compadre*. What is it you have to do, ride off and shoot someone else?"

"I hope not." Ruff glanced toward the cantina, where there seemed to be more noise now, the music louder. "I've got to go, María."

"María!" The voice echoed up the hill from the rear of the cantina. "Where are you, lazy slut?"

"Help me," she said, trying to lift the boy, but Ruff shook his head. "*Cabrón*," she snarled at Ruff as he walked to his gray, swung aboard, and touched the brim of his hat. Then he heeled his horse and walked it out of there, glancing back over his shoulder until he was well out of sight of Zopilote, María, Alfredo, and their troubles.

He rode most of the night, keeping off the trail, riding higher into the foothills, which rose gently. Toward dawn he tumbled from the saddle and made a camp in a small hollow where it would be difficult to approach unheard. He tugged his blanket under his chin and was asleep within minutes.

After a few troubled hours of sleep Justice rose with the sun and headed east again. Now the land began to green. The grass was new and nearly metallic. Here and there he forded a shallow creek. There were more oaks now, cottonwoods in the low spots, only occasional patches of wasteland.

He passed another small pueblo that day, but he stayed wide of it. He had had enough of strangers for a while.

The following day he began to see cattle. Rangy, long-horned stock for the most part. They wore the Slanted T brand of Rancho Trujillo.

An hour before dark he came upon the house itself. A huge spreading mansion. White with red tiles on the roof, an enclosed patio with a fountain and garden behind the house, and before it a grove of sycamores. There was a black iron fence across the road leading to the house, and before it stood a neat little surrey, the wheels painted yellow, drawn by two matched black horses. It all spoke of prosperity and contentment, and Ruff was happy for his friend.

He swung down before the house, standing in front of the long entranceway, which had a tile floor, potted plants in huge ceramic vases, a narrow wrought-iron gate. Ruff wiped the sweat from his forehead and approached the house.

"Who is?"

Ruff looked up to see the tall man in a dark suit and white shirt.

"Ruffin T. Justice," he said. "Señor Trujillo is expecting me."

The butler or whatever he was peered through the iron gate, his eyes expressing unhappy thoughts. "I will see," he said, turning stiffly, and Ruff, grinning, stood looking out across the expanse of yard.

It was a minute before the footsteps echoed on the tile floor of the entranceway and Ruff turned to find not the butler but Carlos Trujillo himself striding toward him, both arms extended, a smile on his lean, handsome, still-youthful face.

"Ruffin T. Justice—by God, it is you," Trujillo said in his booming Texas voice. "And standing out in the sun. Damn Armando." He swung the gate wide, took Ruff's proffered hand between his two, and shook it firmly. "Come in. Come in and cool off, have a drink—oh, you don't drink, that's right—dinner, then. Lemonade."

"A bath," Ruff suggested.

"Hell, yes, a bath—" Trujillo stopped suddenly. They were nearly at the heavy oaken door of the big house when it swung open and two men appeared.

One of them was tall, lean as a snake, with a narrow mustache; the other portly, pink-faced. Justice paused expectantly. There was, he noticed, no warmth at all in either man's expression.

"Ruff Justice, these are Ernesto and Javier . . . Trujillo." Neither man stuck out a hand, although the short one, Javier, nodded. "My uncles," Carlos clarified. "They are just leaving, are you not?" Carlos smiled but there wasn't much warmth in it.

"We are leaving. For now," Ernesto said. He glanced sharply at Ruff and then led off, his stout brother followed him.

"Trouble?" Ruff asked.

"Of the family sort. Nothing to concern yourself with, Ruff. Come in, won't you?"

Carlos led the way into a huge, high-ceilinged room with dark, open beams, a massive fireplace, heavy black Spanish-style furniture, and on the walls sabers, Indian rugs, a coat of arms.

"Very elegant, Carlos."

The younger man blushed slightly. "A little above me, perhaps," he admitted.

"It's big," Justice commented. "For a man alone."

"Yes, well maybe one day I will not be alone."

"You are inviting me to stay?" The voice was feminine, cultivated, and Ruff turned to see the woman standing there, smiling deeply. She was young, elegant, poised. She crossed the room, clutching a white handkerchief in one hand. She wore a black dress that dusted the floor as she moved toward the men, and a high Spanish comb in her raven-black hair.

"You have company, Carlos," she said, extending her hand to Trujillo, who took it only briefly, dropping it too quickly. The woman smiled again. Lord, she was a proud one. Proud and self-controlled. And very, very beautiful.

"May I present Elena María Cortes," Trujillo said, stammering a little. "Elena, this is my American friend, Mr. Ruffin T. Justice."

"So," she said, her black eyes flashing, "this is the one."

Carlos looked a little embarrassed. "I've told Elena something about you."

"Not too much, I hope," Ruff answered. His eyes were still on the lovely Elena.

"I hope not too," Carlos answered. "Come out on the patio, won't you both?"

Carlos led the way into the walled patio. There the fountain babbled away merrily. There were larks in the pepper trees that shaded the area. Carlos sat at the round, cane table that stood near the door. Ruff held Elena's chair and she settled in with a warm, grateful smile.

"I guess I'd better tell you what's been happening, why Elena is here, why she's going with us."

"Going with us?" Ruff sat upright, folding his hands on the table. "You know what kind of drive this is going to be, Carlos. I've brought trouble with me. There's an American who doesn't want these cows reaching New Mexico. There's Chato Chavez out prowling. We've got Apaches and hard weather, dry trails and outlaws. You can't be serious about this."

"It has to be, Ruffin. I have given my word." Carlos smiled apologetically, spreading his hands. "Elena must travel north, and there is no other way for her to go."

"There's got to be a better way than with a herd of cattle across that country."

"What safer way, Mr. Justice?" Elena asked. "There will be many men with us, no?"

"Not enough, if Chavez shows."

"Perhaps not, but it is imperative that I reach the United States in the next ten days."

Ruff was silent a moment, thinking. Behind him the fountain splashed away. "You two aren't . . . engaged or something?"

Carlos shook his head negatively. "Elena is merely a friend of our family. There is nothing between us. She is however, engaged, and this is the reason she must travel north."

"I am going to marry an American. Mr. William Dobbs of El Paso, Texas," Elena recited.

"Then just why doesn't Mr. William Dobbs come down here and collect you?" Ruff asked, his annoyance showing.

"Unfortunately that is impossible. Mr. Dobbs has a complicated business schedule. It must be myself who travels."

"You could wait until this country has cooled down a little," Ruff suggested.

"No. It must be soon," Elena said firmly.

Ruff glanced at Carlos, who shrugged.

"You'd better explain, Elena."

"Very well." Elena's features stiffened slightly, then relaxed again. She looked down at the table, at her hands, which rested there. "It is a marriage of necessity, Mr. Justice."

"Elena's people are gone, Ruff," Carlos put in. "Her father's rancho is deeply mortgaged. Her father was, unfortunately, a gambling man."

"He was a fine man," Elena put in hastily.

Carlos agreed. "He was a hell of a man. But he did have that single fault. After Don Ricardo was shot in a card game, his debts began to surface. There were a hell of a lot of them."

"The horses went first, Mr. Justice. The finest horses, of Arabian blood. Then the cattle. Finally the furniture of the house. Now I have only the rancho, and it too is deeply burdened."

"The moneylenders in this country have never heard of usury, Ruff. No matter what Elena does, it's not enough."

"So you're going to marry your way out of it?"

"What else is there to do, Mr. Ruff Justice?" Elena asked with some heat.

"I don't know." Ruff looked at Carlos, who guessed at what was in his mind.

"I don't have it, Ruff. One reason I took you up on this is that I'm desperately in need of money myself. The beef market down here is very limited. There just aren't any people around."

It was the same situation that had prevailed in Texas before the war. The more cattle a man had, the poorer he was said to be. There wasn't a market in the days before the railroads. The long drives were a chancy business. Cattle were routinely slaughtered for hides and tallow alone, the meat left to the critters.

"His uncles, you see," Elena began.

Carlos shot her a hard glance and then, sighing, told the story himself. "Didn't want to burden you with this. Uncles Ernesto and Javier, however, are set against me. They figured that they should have inherited this land, this house. It's rare for a woman to have inherited, but my mother did. Then when she died suddenly, it was mine. Ernesto and Javier have been trying to take Rancho Trujillo ever since."

"They have challenged him in the courts," Elena said, "and our friend Carlos hasn't the money to see it through."

"Not only that, there is a stipulation that I share profits with Ernesto and Javier. They each get ten percent. Well, there haven't been any damned profits and they're accusing me of mismanagement. They may well win the case, Ruff, if they can prove that."

Justice nodded, looking at the woman, at his friend. They were in the same boat, it seemed. They had cattle that must be driven north. Elena had to find and marry her Texas man. Carlos needed money badly. Ruff Justice had nothing to lose personally, but there were a lot of reservation Indians who would be going hungry if they didn't get some beef damned soon, and a hungry man is apt to be a violent one.

He looked at them both again, grinned and asked, "When do we leave?"

4

Carlos had neglected to tell Ruff a few things. Chief among these was the fact that he had almost no help. The vaqueros had been let go one at a time as the money dwindled. The Rancho Trujillo had a compliment of exactly three men. One was an ancient, mustached man named Miguel, who had worked for Carlos' grandfather and then his father. He was tanned like leather, wrinkled, lean, and bent. He had a constitution of whipcord, but Ruff doubted he was up to a drive like this one.

Besides Miguel, there were just two other men: Wilfredo, who had been with the rancho for twenty years and was foreman now that Miguel was on the sundown side; and Wilfredo's son, a flashy kid of twenty or so who strutted about cocksure of himself as only the very young can be.

His name was Pablo and he seemed to spend most of his time fondling his low-slung Remington pistol and leering at Elena.

"It's not enough, Carlos," Justice told him. "We'll need some men."

"The money, Ruff . . ." Carlos spread his hands helplessly.

"You'll have money at the other end, Carlos. You should be able to find some hands to work for a promise." The local economy didn't look all that good.

"There is no one. My men have all dispersed."

"I saw a town on the way down here."

"There is no one there. Only Jumano Indians. They have never worked cattle, Ruff."

"Will they work for you?"

"They might, yes, but there's no money and they're inexperienced." Carlos was suffering from nerves. His mind was holding him back.

Ruff told him that. "Most men don't lift up their heads and see that there's nothing physical actually holding them back from what they want to do. It's the mind, Carlos. Let's have some positive thinking!" That happy speech finished, Ruff slapped Carlos on the shoulder and got to his own brooding.

It was bad, and looking worse. Bad country, bad conditions, no able help. He swallowed some of his own advice and looked for the bright side. It was getting difficult to find.

"I'll take the old man and ride on over to the pueblo," Ruff suggested. "We'll see what kind of help's available. Meantime, you and Wilfredo and his kid might as well start bunching those cattle up. We're going, Carlos. One way or the other, we're going north."

With Miguel Ruff rode toward the pueblo that morning. "They are very strange men, these Jumanos," the old man told him. "They are known as cutthroats. They will do nothing a man orders them to do. Yet they are loyal and will share their last bit of food."

"Doesn't sound real promising," Ruff said. "There's no other place around where we could round up some men?"

"No, Ruff Justice. Not for many miles."

Ruff nodded. They would just have to try the Jumanos, then.

The land was wide and treeless. Sparse brown grass covered the baked earth. Far off, a crow wheeled and cawed through the air. Miguel rode soberly beside Ruff, his gnarled, leathery hand lightly gripping the reins of the sorrel gelding he rode. There was little conversation between the men until they were within sight of the Jumano pueblo.

"There is a store where the men gather to drink," Miguel said. "That is where we must go."

"All right."

"It can be very bad, Ruff Justice, with strangers." Miguel's seamed face reflected just how bad he thought it could get.

"You want to wait here?"

"Me!" Miguel was offended. "I am working for the Rancho Trujillo. I do not let someone else do my work."

He must have been a hell of a lot of man in his prime, Ruff thought. The back of Miguel was rigid now, his eyes glittering as they rode into the pueblo, seeing dark eyes staring at them from the shadows. The sun beat down on the main street, which had deep ruts baked into it by summer suns. The buildings were all of adobe. All three of them. On all of them the plaster had peeled off, revealing the adobe bricks beneath.

Miguel nodded at the first building on their right. "It is there, Mr. Justice."

They pulled up before the store and swung down, Ruff waiting before the door for Miguel to join him, his legs working stiffly. Ruff glanced inside and then pushed through into the sour-smelling, dark interior of the Jumano store.

They sat on the counter, on barrels, on stacks of blankets, their eyes attentive and menacing, their dark faces expressionless, as Justice entered, Miguel at his shoulder.

They all appeared half-intoxicated and Ruff saw a bottle of mescal change hands. No one moved. They simply sat and stared. Justice thought of a rattlesnake den, and if he wasn't careful, he might end up with exactly the same result a man got trampling on rattlers.

A heavy Indian with red eyes and three extra

chins got up from his cracker-barrel perch and started toward Ruff. He was a head taller than Ruff and twice as wide. There was a malicious glee in his eyes.

"Get out," he said in Spanish. "This is not your place."

"I've come to offer you money," Justice answered.

The big Jumano halted a stride away from Justice and crossed his arms on his massive chest. "Good. Then give it to me." He laughed, looking around to see that his humor was appreciated.

"It's work I've come to offer you. All of you." Justice looked from one man to the next. "If you're not interested, then I'll be on my way."

"What kind of work?" the big one growled.

"A cattle drive. The Rancho Trujillo is driving some cattle up to the United States. We can use some men."

"For this you want Jumanos?"

"For this I want some men who are willing to work," Justice answered.

The big Indian had eased forward a little more. Now Ruff could smell the sweat of him, the sour mescal odor of his breath.

"You know who I am?" the Indian asked.

"No, and it doesn't have much to do with anything."

"I am Cosacha."

"I am Ruff Justice," the scout replied quietly.

"Cosacha does not work for Spanish. Does not work for English."

"Fine. Go sit down, then. Maybe some of the other men would like to work."

"For how much?" a lean man wearing a blue cotton shirt asked.

"One American dollar a day."

"Didn't you hear Cosacha?" the big man persisted. "I said I do not work."

"I heard you," Ruff said, feeling the pit of his stomach begin to tighten, his eyes start to go dry and hard as adrenaline pumped through his system.

"You know why not?" Cosacha pushed his big ugly face toward Ruff's. "Because all are women, not men. Women! The Spanish are women, the English are women."

"Think what you like, Cosacha. If there's anyone else . . ."

"You are talking to me," Cosacha shouted, his eyes bulging out like a toad's.

"Not anymore, *amigo*. I'm talking to whoever wants to work." Ruff leveled his icy-blue eyes on Cosacha, delivering a message that Cosacha wasn't willing to accept.

"Who would be boss? You?" Cosacha asked.

"That's right. I am the boss, Cosacha."

"Tough enough to boss the Jumanos? You are tough enough to boss Cosacha?" The Indian's hand darted out and caught Ruff's shirtfront suddenly, bunching it as he drew Ruff nearer. Behind Cosacha someone snickered.

"Let's find out," Ruff said coldly, and Cosacha threw back his head and roared with laughter.

"Yes, English, let us find out." Then, still holding Ruff's shirt, the Indian let fly a looping right hand from out of nowhere; it landed on Justice's skull and the lights blinked on in back of his eyes.

Justice was slammed back against the upright behind him. The breath was jolted out of his lungs. His legs were wobbly. There was the salt taste of blood in his mouth. And Cosacha coming in.

The big man came on like a grizzly, massive fists bunched, his tiny malevolent eyes gleaming. Justice pushed away from the upright and launched himself at the Indian. His head drove into the Jumano's belly and Justice kept churning. They crashed into a pile of crates and went down in a heap.

Justice felt himself thrown aside by a massive arm, and he saw the big fist arc in again. This time he was ready and he rolled aside, the fist just grazing his temple.

Ruff came to his feet, kicking aside a splintered crate. As Cosacha waded in, Ruff stabbed out twice with his left hand, jolting back the Indian's head, bringing tears to his eyes. As Cosacha tried another wild left, Ruff countered with a right, which landed solidly on his jaw. It wasn't enough to keep the Indian from coming in.

Ruff ducked a heavy right hand hook thrown by Cosacha and went inside, hammering away at Cosacha's ribs with lefts and rights. Cosacha locked his huge arms around Ruff's chest and lifted him, squeezing him until his lungs felt as if they would burst, his spine snap.

Justice kicked out, catching shin and knees, but Cosacha kept his grip. Ruff's head was swimming with crimson fire, and angrily he brought his knee up, catching the Indian in the groin. Cosacha moaned, his eyes bulging out still farther, but he held on tenaciously.

Justice got his right arm free and slammed his forearm against the big man's nose, spattering them both with blood as Cosacha, with a bellow of pain, fell back. Justice stayed on top of him, throwing two rights to Cosacha's damaged nose.

From the corner of his eye Ruff caught sight of Miguel. The old Mexican had drawn his gun and he now held it carelessly in hand, his eyes on the rest of the Jumanos.

"Kill him, Cosacha," someone yelled cheerfully, and Cosacha determined to do his best.

He reached behind him and came up with an ax handle. As Justice came in, the Indian hammered down with it. Justice was just able to jerk to the right, causing the murderous blow to miss by inches.

Before Cosacha could lift the ax handle again, Justice was in on top of him, his hand clamped around Cosacha's wrist. Cosacha whistled a left past Ruff's nose and Justice countered savagely, his right-hand shot slamming into the Indian's windpipe.

Cosacha fell back, gagging horribly, clutching his throat. Justice was all over him like a big cat, two rights digging into the Indian's wind, a left coming over the top to glance off the big man's skull.

Cosacha looked tired now, vaguely puzzled. He had his hands up before his face, holding them loosely like paws. Ruff could hear the big man's ragged breathing, see from his slack jaw that he was weary.

Justice was far from it. Some savage fury had taken hold of him. The world outside didn't exist. Nothing existed but the dark, ugly face before him, and it had to be destroyed. Ruff's whole existence seemed to depend on it, and he got to work.

A left dug into the Indian's liver. Ruff's boot toe caught Cosacha's ankle, and the big man staggered away, throwing punches with both hands. He was in a fury, trying to take Ruff's head off, but there was nothing behind the blows. Justice bobbed away from two of them and then went to the Indian's wind again.

Cosacha doubled up with pain and Justice finished it. As the big man folded up, Ruff brought an upper-cut from the floor. It landed solidly, all of Ruff's weight behind it, all of his anger, and Cosacha flew back, his mouth streaming blood. He fell into the counter, the small of his back catching the corner. Cosacha never felt it. He was already out cold. He stayed on his feet for a minute and then slowly slid to the floor to sit leaning against the counter, his battered face slack and peaceful.

Justice stepped back, his chest heaving as he gasped for breath. His hands were cramped into tight balls. He turned his head and spat out a mouthful of blood.

Miguel still stood there, pistol in hand, his old eyes sharp and ready. None of the other Jumanos had moved. None tried it now.

"The offer is still open," Justice said. There was no

answer, no response at all, just a row of dark, scarred faces watching him.

Justice snatched up his hat and pulled it on, tossing his hair back. Cosacha moaned, and Ruff, glancing at him, saw an eyelid flicker, saw an involuntary twitch begin in the big man's arm.

"Let's get out of here, Miguel."

"I think yes. I will go first, Mr. Ruff Justice, if you will watch our backs."

The old man smiled and Ruff grinned painfully in return. Miguel had been in some situations in his time, obviously. Miguel turned and went to the saloon door, peering out into the sunlight. "I think we may go," he said, and Ruff started backing toward him, his hand resting on his Colt.

"Wait!" It was Cosacha who called out. The big man tried to stand and found he couldn't. Finally, grasping the edge of the counter, he pulled his great bulk upright.

"Wait a minute, Justice. How many men do you want?"

Ruff could only gape at the Indian. "What kind of joke is this, Cosacha?"

"No joke. We need work." The big man was leaning heavily on the counter, bracing himself with an elbow. Now he sucked in a deep breath and stood on his two feet. His broad, ugly face was blood-streaked, battered.

"You didn't need it a while ago," Ruff said.

"Maybe no. I asked could you boss Cosacha. I did not think you could. Now the fight is over. You have beat me. All right—I am coming to work if you want me. So are these lazy Jumanos here. Except Juan, who has a new wife." He turned and winked at Juan, who seemed vastly relieved.

"Be at Rancho Trujillo in the morning. Do you have horses? At least two apiece."

"Those we do not have we shall get," Cosacha said

in a way that let Ruff know he didn't want to ask where the horses were coming from.

"A dollar a day. I'm the boss. If that's all right, you come along."

"We will be there," Cosacha said again.

Justice nodded, but when he left, he was careful nevertheless to back from the room, something that seemed to amuse Cosacha.

Miguel was astride his sorrel, handing Ruff his reins. Justice swung aboard, the Mexican's questioning eyes on him. "Well?" the Rancho Trujillo foreman asked.

"We have some men. I think."

"Cosacha said it is so?"

"He said so." Inside the store the buzz of conversation had begun again as if nothing had happened. Ruff turned the gray's head away from the hitching rail and they started up the hard-packed street, scattering a flock of yellow chickens that had been scratching at the dry earth expectantly.

"They will come, then," Miguel said. "Cosacha will not lie. No Jumano will lie."

"Cut your throat but not lie, is that it?" Ruff asked with a grin. He was dabbing at his mouth with the corner of his scarf.

Miguel laughed. "That is a Jumano for you. They will fight *for* you as they fought against you. It is their way, Mr. Ruff Justice. They are very fierce, very loyal."

Ruff only grunted. He hoped that what Miguel said was true. If it wasn't, they would have much trouble going north. They would have trouble anyway. The Jumanos weren't vaqueros; they didn't know cattle. At least, he thought, if it came to a fight with Dunweather—and it might to get those steers across the border—he had some fighters.

He did indeed have some fighters. Ruff spat out some blood, and with his head still ringing from

Cosacha's blows, he followed Miguel across the parched land toward Rancho Trujillo.

"Look, Mr. Ruff Justice," Miguel said, pulling up, and Ruff lifted his eyes to follow Miguel's gnarled brown finger. There were six horsemen watching them. Vaqueros in fancy dress. Tight jackets, flaring, slash-cuffed pants, wide sombreros. Much silver on their saddles and bridles.

"Who the hell are they?"

"Ernesto Trujillo's men," Miguel said through his teeth. "But what the *patróns'* brother's men are doing here I cannot say."

"Let's ask them," Ruff suggested.

Miguel glanced at him sharply, then slowly he smiled. "Why not? This is our lucky day, I think."

But before they had reached the six Mexicans, they had turned their horses and disappeared through the oaks along the creek bottom. Whatever Carlos' brother wanted, they wouldn't discover that day.

"I think," Carlos told Ruff later as they sat in the patio sipping lemonade, "that Ernesto has been taking cattle. I have no proof of this, but I believe it is so."

"He thinks they belong to him?" Ruff took another drink of his lemonade. It stung the cuts in his mouth.

"Yes." Carlos shrugged. "He thinks he has a right to them. He thinks the house should be his and all of the land. But"—he smiled—"it is only the cattle that he can steal easily."

"You'll have to do something about Ernesto and Javier sooner or later, Carlos. You won't have any peace until you do."

"I know this," Carlos said with a sigh. He settled back in his chair. "Because they know I need the money, they take the cattle, hoping to accelerate my poverty. They feel aggrieved. It is most unusual. Most *unnatural* for this property to have come down to me, the way they see it."

"I don't know a thing about Mexican law, but I

know the Mexican people," Ruff said. "To will the estate to your mother broke an unwritten law, didn't it?"

"Oh, yes. Always it is the sons who receive the property. The women, if they are lucky, receive a little money and a place to stay."

"But your mother inherited. Why is that?"

"Why?" Carlos smiled thinly again. "Because, Ruff, Ernesto and Javier are two of the biggest bastards that ever walked the earth, and my grandfather knew it!"

5

Ruff Justice sat soaking in the tub. Outside the open veranda window the sky was going pink and deep rose. The breeze was warm. Doves winged homeward against the sundown sky.

The water was hot, soothing. His body still ached from his discussion with Cosacha, but the bath was doing wonders. The door popped open and Carlos' house servant came in with another bucket of heated water from the kitchen.

"Easy now," Ruff told the kid as he started to pour. "Let's not boil anything I might have use for."

The kid grinned at Justice, flashing good white teeth. "Will you need more water, Mr. Ruff Justice?"

"No, that'll do it. Looks like we're full up."

"I have put a towel on the chair there."

"Bueno. Thanks."

The kid made a little bow and then left, pulling the door shut softly, and Ruff closed his eyes, leaning back in the hot tub. He let the water soothe him, erase the tension. He was half-asleep, his mind furnishing him with a waking dream. He was in a long-ago place with a Crow woman named Four Dove. The pines were tall and dark, swaying in the breeze. The brook burbled past, singing atavistic songs . . .

There was someone in the room. Ruff fought back the impulse to come upright, to make any quick movement. Slowly he lifted one eyelid, his muscles bunching, ready to hurl Ruff into action. There was no need.

"Good evening, Elena. What are you doing here?"

She came forward, dressed in a white satin dress that followed the flow of her breasts and hips entrancingly. There was a tiny, mocking smile on her red lips.

"I wanted to talk to you. I did not know you were in the bath."

"I guess you figured all that water they were bringing in here was to fill the fishbowl."

"*¿Qué?*" Elena tilted her head and smiled, all innocence. She knew now that Justice was in the tub, but she wasn't making any noticeable effort to leave. She sat down on the nearest chair, looking at Justice in a way that caused some submerged excitement.

"What is it, Elena?"

"I want to know why you are ignoring me, Ruff."

"I haven't been ignoring you."

"You speak to me, but it is all so formal—like with Carlos."

"You'd rather have me gaping at you like young Pablo."

"He is a pup," she said disparagingly.

"Don't go treating him like one, or you're liable to find you've made some trouble," Ruff warned her. But Elena didn't want to talk about the swaggering young Pablo. She scooted her chair nearer and rested a hand on Ruff's knee.

"You have not answered me. Why do you not treat me like a woman? You do not look at me like a man looks at a woman, you do not speak to me that way."

"It's simple, you're engaged to another man. I love a woman, Elena, a good healthy, laughing, loving woman, but I've got this odd little quirk—I don't make a try for another man's woman."

"You are a moralist, Ruff Justice?"

"Not exactly," he admitted, "but there's rules, Elena María, and one of them says you don't go after another man's woman. Especially not when they're going to be married."

"Married! But to a man I do not even know. He is old, Ruff Justice, and very ugly."

"Then you should have chosen another."

"Don't you know"—her eyes searched his—"I did not choose this one? It was given to me to do by my family, and I will do it. Don't you understand how these marriages are made with us?"

Ruff felt a little smaller. He *had* forgotten about arranged marriages. About young women traded off to rich men for the benefit of the family fortune. That was what this marriage to William Dobbs was, pure and simple. And he had the feeling that she would make him a good wife. Spanish women are known for their fidelity, for their sense of honor, which doesn't allow indiscretions. She would make him a good and faithful wife . . . but now she was just a young woman, barely out of her teens, who hadn't much of a life to look forward to.

"I am sorry I have troubled your bath," she said with a quick, weak smile. Then she rose, lifting her hand from his knee. She smiled again and turned away, sweeping out of the room, leaving the door open behind her.

Ruff washed up quickly and climbed out of the tub—the enjoyment of it had gone.

Elena was absent from supper that evening, and Ruff and Carlos faced each other across the long mahogany table, eating in silence. Justice was wearing a borrowed white shirt and black suit belonging to Carlos. As tall as Ruff was, the suit was a little long for him. But he figured he would be in his working clothes for a long while after this evening, and he had the taste on this evening for fine crystal, fine silver, pressed clothes . . . and the soft conversation of a woman.

"It is only a headache that troubles Elena," Carlos said, and Ruff nodded.

"Everything ready in the morning?" Justice asked.

"If your vaqueros show up," Trujillo said with a worried expression.

"They'll show up, but after that I don't know—Cosacha is volatile, and all of the Jumanos might be unpredictable."

"Miguel says they will follow your orders now."

"I hope so." But how far could he trust the Indians?

"*¿Señor?*" It was the butler, Armando. His face was drawn with concern. He bent low and whispered something into Carlos Trujillo's ear.

"Damn," Carlos breathed, throwing his napkin down angrily.

"What is it?"

"You'll see. Have them come in, Armando." The butler turned away and Carlos said to Ruff, "My brothers are back."

In a moment Ernesto and the plump Javier entered, the butler tagging along behind them. Their leather heels clicked on the tile floor. Their faces were grim, but their eyes bright with triumph. Ernesto had a document in his hand, one with a red wax seal on it, and the lean mustached uncle tossed it on the table, nearly upsetting Carlos' wine.

"From the magistrate, Nephew," the snakelike Ernesto said. He spared a raking glance for Ruff Justice.

Carlos opened the document, read it once hastily, then again more slowly. Finally he lowered it, his eyes hard and cold. "Well, that is that."

"What's the matter, Carlos?" Ruff asked.

"An order from the magistrate's office. No property of any sort is to be removed from Rancho Trujillo until the pending ownership case is decided."

"Including livestock?"

"Specifically including livestock," Carlos said, looking at his uncle, who returned his savage gaze. "It is too bad that others are not similarly prohibited from removing cattle from this land."

"What does that remark mean?" Ernesto said, stiffening.

"It means what you think it does, Uncle Ernesto. Your vaqueros are not ghosts. They have been seen on my property."

"You are accusing me?" There was a slow, ugly joy building in the eyes of Ernesto Trujillo, and Justice thought he knew why. He wanted badly to eliminate Carlos, and a man killed in a duel was legally killed in Mexico. Carlos was rising to the bait, but Justice intervened.

"He was just making a statement." Justice stroked his mustache with his napkin and then rose, walking to the other end of the table.

"What have you to do with this, you—whoever you are?" Ernesto's eyes were blazing.

"I am only a friend."

"Ruff, I appreciate this, but you don't have to take a hand." Carlos started to rise, but Justice rested a hand on his friend's shoulder.

"No? It appears I'm already involved, Carlos."

"I have not finished discussing matters with my nephew," Ernesto said. He and Justice were standing with their eyes bare inches apart, and neither man showed any inclination to back down.

"You've finished. You've come and delivered your papers. He's read them. Now it's time for you to go."

"You will not throw me out of my father's house," Ernesto said heatedly.

"That's the point, isn't it?" Ruff said. "This isn't your father's house anymore. It's not yours. It belongs to Carlos."

"For now. But not for long," Ernesto said. He was trembling with anger.

Javier stood to one side, looking anything but confident. Sweat glistened on his pink forehead.

"We'll see about that," Ruff said. "For now—get out."

"Damn you! Damn the two of you." Ernesto leveled a finger at Carlos. "This is not over. Soon you will be where you belong, back in the United States and off of this property." He started away and then stopped to add, "If you have any idea of going ahead with this plan of yours, let me tell you this. Tomorrow the Rurales will arrive to make sure that you do not move a single steer from this land. My vaqueros are even now riding the property line, and they have orders to shoot any man who tries to leave Rancho Trujillo with any of its property."

Then he was gone, stalking toward the door, Javier scurrying along after him, still mopping his perspiring brow.

Carlos sat stiffly in his chair, staring straight ahead, his hand covering the restraining order. "That's it. We're finished. I'm sorry, Ruff."

"Finished? Carlos, a man's not finished until they've begun shoveling that cold earth onto his face."

"But we can't go now—you heard Ernesto."

"And if you don't go? It's true, isn't it, that you don't have the money to fight what they're trying to do to you?"

"Yes, but . . ." Carlos just shook his head wearily.

"There's only one way to come by that money, Carlos. If you don't want to go, then we won't. I'll come up with some other scheme for getting beef to Fort Sumner. I don't know just what, but I will. If you don't want to go, fine. I can understand it. It's risking jail, your life even. I can't make the decision for you, but I can remind you that if you sit here, you're sunk. And so, I guess, are Elena's people."

"And you?"

"I don't matter."

"The soldiers who are counting on you. The reservation Indians. The people who will be in the way if those Indians come off the reservation."

Ruff made no answer. He had said all he meant to say. The final decision was Carlos'. When he had made it, he rose from his chair—a little shakily, it seemed.

"We will go," the young man said.

"All right. Tonight, then. The sooner the better. If your uncles are going to have the Rurales in here tomorrow, it has to be tonight."

They couldn't get into a gun battle with the Mexican police. As for the rest of it, they would have to take their chances. Ernesto had his vaqueros out there, and that meant bloodshed, unless they could come up with a way to slip past them.

"We have not got the Jumanos to help us."

"We'll get them. We'll send someone or I'll go myself."

"All right." Carlos had made up his mind. Now again he was determined if not exactly confident. "I'll have Elena's wagon packed, have Miguel, Wilfredo, and Pablo start preparations for the drive. There shouldn't be much time involved. But the herd will have to be smaller than we had hoped."

"That can't be helped. We'll take what you have herded up and begin as soon as possible." At night. With inexperienced men. Through a ring of guards. Ruff allowed all of those thoughts to lodge only fleetingly in his mind. Concentrating on the negative would get them nowhere.

Justice was already taking off his tie, unbuttoning his shirt, as he made for the staircase, hearing Carlos call out to Armando.

"What is it?" Elena asked.

She had appeared out of her bedroom, clutching a wrapper to her breast. Her dark hair was loose around her shoulders. With her makeup scrubbed off, dressed like this, she looked very young and vulnerable. And damned appealing.

Justice told her. "We're leaving tonight. Pack up what you can."

"Tonight!" Elena's face drained of blood. "There is trouble?"

"There will be if we don't get moving. Get yourself dressed and don't waste any time fussing with your hair." He had spoken harshly, and Elena's eyes reflected hurt and confusion. Justice smiled and stretched out a hand, touching her silky, raven-black hair. "It looks fine just the way it is," he added softly.

Justice was dressed and packed in fifteen minutes. Going downstairs, saddlebags slung over his shoulder, he met Carlos.

"Miguel has gone to talk to the Jumanos and bring them back."

"All right." Ruff noticed a house servant with a trunk on his back crossing the room. The open door revealed a wagon standing ready before the house. "I'm going to go out and have a look at things, Carlos. When the Jumanos get here, put them to work gathering cattle. But let's not spend a lot of time at it. We're going to have to get out of here in the next couple of hours with whatever we've gathered."

"If we can get out," Carlos said.

"That is what I intend to find out right now."

Outside, all was still. It was eerie, considering the entire rancho was on the move. But the cattle were being held half a mile away, and the work inside the house was inaudible. Ruff stood beneath the big stars for a minute, letting his eyes adjust to the darkness, listening to the hooting of a distant owl. Then, carrying his rifle and saddlebags, he walked to the corral, saddled the gray horse, and started westward.

He kept to the oaks where possible, but there were few trees a quarter of a mile on and he moved cautiously along the bottoms, pausing every little while to listen and watch.

Where the road crossed the boundary he found them: two vaqueros squatting beside a small cone of red fire. Just a cheerful little picnic. Ruff smiled sardonically. Slipping from the saddle, he worked his way through the rocks. He went cautiously—although these two seemed to be fools, it wasn't necessarily so. There could have been some kind of trap laid.

There wasn't. Not here, not now. Justice emerged from the rocks and walked toward the two Mexicans, rifle leveled at them.

"Don't shoot." Neither rose from his crouch. They simply stared at the muzzle of that .56, eyes wide.

Ruff spoke to the man on his right. "Take that lariat and tie your *compadre* up."

"*Sí, señor*. Do not shoot."

Ruff did his best to look as if he would shoot if there was a mistake. "Make it tight, *amigo*," he said, and the vaquero nodded, tightening the rope he had looped around his friend's wrists.

"Now you can start on yourself," Ruff said when he was finished. "Sit down and tie your ankles together."

The vaquero did as he was told, and when Ruff walked toward him to check the knots, he found them tight. "Hands behind your back, *hombre*," Justice said, and the vaquero complied.

Justice quickly tied the man's hands. Then, lifting their weapons, he shooed their horses on out of there and hotfooted it back to where the grey stood waiting impatiently.

Ruff worked up the boundary, finding no one else. Turning back, he rode south, again finding no one. The Trujillos had placed a lot of trust in those two vaqueros, it seemed.

He rode through the night, finding Carlos waiting for him when he returned. Trujillo was in range clothes, and he was ready to ride. Carlos looked unhappy about things, but his youthful face was determined.

"Elena?"

"She is ready, Ruff. She's in the dining room."

"The Jumanos?"

They had arrived, Carlos told him. They were bunching the cattle under Wilfredo's direction.

"I'll head up there and find them," Ruff said. Briefly he told Carlos about the two vaqueros. "The main road now is the safest way. Grab Elena and let's get moving."

He didn't have to grab her. She emerged from the shadows, satchel in hand, wearing a hooded cape. She too looked grim but determined.

"Ready?" Ruff asked.

"If you will help me up," Elena said a little stiffly, and Justice gave her a hand up into the wagon box. Armando came out, closing the gate behind him. The butler was wearing jeans and a flannel shirt, both obviously new, both ill-fitting.

"I have sent Manuel and Olga home, with your thanks, sir," the butler reported. "The house is empty."

"Thank you, Armando," Carlos said. He stood for a moment, looking at the darkened ranch house, then he nodded thoughtfully and smiled. "Let's go, Mr. Justice."

Ruff mounted and rode northward toward the cattle. They were bawling and milling, unhappy about being moved at night. They would be unhappier yet soon. The grass was sparse out on the desert, the water insufficient.

Ruff found Pablo first. "We're ready to go, start stringing them out, Pablo. We'll be taking the main road."

"When my father tells me," the kid said. Then, damn him, he smiled challengingly, his white teeth flashing. Ruff noticed he had his hand resting on his low-slung Remington.

"There isn't going to be time for any of that, Pablo. You understand me? We've got enough enemies on our trail without man-child games. Do you understand me?"

"Sure. I understand you," Pablo said, but he was still smiling, inviting trouble. Ruff knew the type, knew them too well. Swaggering, challenging the world in their youthful belief in their own immortality. Maybe Pablo had read too many dime novels. He was begging for it, but Ruff wasn't playing.

He turned the horse and walked it away, knowing that in Pablo's mind he had backed down.

Wilfredo was pushing three cows up from an oak-shadowed gulley toward the herd. Justice told him, "We're ready."

"All right. You will talk to your Indians?" Wilfredo wiped his forehead with the back of his sleeve. "They seem to want to hear your orders before they will do anything."

"Where are they?"

"Back there." Wilfredo nodded toward the gulley.

"I'll talk to them. See what you can do to get this herd into motion."

He found Cosacha squatting on the ground beside a big steer. What he was doing wasn't apparent, and he gave it up as Justice appeared through the star-shadowed trees.

"We are going, Ruff Justice?"

"If you're ready," Ruff replied, looking at the big, lumpy face of the Jumano.

"We are ready, but we were waiting for you. There are five of us only. Antonio could not be found."

"All right. Have two of your men get behind the herd and start pushing them forward. Slowly, Cosacha. No excitement, understand?"

"I understand."

"We'll have to move as quietly as possible. There are some vaqueros around who don't want us leaving."

Cosacha received this news almost joyfully. "If they wish to fight, then we will show them something, eh?"

"Yes, but we don't want a fight if we can avoid it. These cattle would scatter all over hell at the first sound of gunfire. Let's keep it quiet, but stay alert. Cosacha, I want you to listen to me. If Miguel or

Wilfredo tell you to do something, do it. Those men know cattle. They know them better than I ever will. You listen to them, all right?"

"And the pup?" Cosacha asked, smiling darkly.

"Pablo—just leave him alone."

"He fancies himself, Ruff Justice."

"He's young, he doesn't know any better."

"Yes." Cosacha rubbed his jaw. "I too was young once and knew no better. An old man taught me the truth very quickly."

"Leave it to someone else. Now let's stop jawin' and get working."

"Yes, Ruff Justice." Cosacha walked to his horse and swung heavily aboard.

Ruff watched him for a minute and then turned the gray toward the point.

The cattle were stringing out toward the west. Ruff saw Miguel slapping at the laggards with his rope. Across the herd he could see Pablo and his father. Dust rose in the night, the clopping of hooves mingled with the clacking of horns. The stars were bright and somewhere far to the north lay Fort Sumner.

6

They drove on through the night, and when the rising sun sketched shadows out before them, they were twenty miles from Rancho Trujillo. No shots had been fired. The vaqueros of the Trujillo brothers had either been fooled or had decided they had no taste for fighting. Still, they couldn't be discounted and Ruff continually slowed to watch the backtrail.

"The grass will run out very soon," Carlos said to Justice. "It would be best to stop and let them graze here, no?"

Ruff's own thought was that it would be best to put as many miles as possible between themselves and possible pursuit, but it was Carlos' herd and Ruff recognized that if they expected the cattle to make it across the desert, they would have to be as strong and rested as possible.

"Is there water nearby?" Justice asked.

"The Jamale Tanks," Carlos said, vaguely indicating something to the north. "It might well be brackish by this time of the year, but perhaps not."

"Your choice, Carlos. I can't make those kinds of decisions."

"All right. Let's push them on another five miles. Let them graze, but keep them up. I'll send someone over to the tanks. If that's no good, then we might as well go on the fifteen miles to the Carrizo Creek."

As it turned out, they went ahead to the Carrizo. Miguel had ridden to the tanks and reported the water low and alkaline. The herd, still not broken to

61

the trail, was balky and hard to handle. Now and then one of them would break out and try to head back home.

By the time they reached the Carrizo, the herd was loose at the knees, exhausted, and contrary. The men were feeling no better. Tempers were short after only a day of this, and Ruff didn't like it.

Two of the Jumanos got into a fistfight and Cosacha had to break it up. "They already miss the women and the mescal," he told Justice.

"They'll stick, won't they?" Ruff asked.

"Yes, Ruff Justice. They will stay if Cosacha tells them to stay."

The cattle lined the shallow, sun-glittering creek as dusk settled. Armando, stiff from the day aboard the wagon, already had a fire going, coffee brewing. Ruff wandered through the camp, speaking to the Jumanos. He caught sight of Miguel sitting stiff and proud aboard his horse, watching the herd drink. Pablo stood nearby, his shoulder against his horse, rolling a cigarette. His eyes were dark and mocking. Ruff ignored him.

"No trouble yet," Carlos said cheerfully. "Perhaps we have overestimated the difficulties."

"Perhaps," Ruff said, though he thought nothing of the sort.

Wilfredo had organized the men into watches and the first group of night herders was eating hastily even before the sun disappeared in a blaze of glory behind the willows that flanked the river.

Justice saw Elena near the fire, sipping at a tin mug full of coffee, and he started that way himself.

"Join you?" he asked, and Elena turned fire-bright eyes to him.

"I would be very pleased, Ruff."

Justice poured himself a cup and sat on the fallen log beside her. The cattle were settling down wearily, the shadows long, the sun only a faint reddish memory on the western sky. Armando was stirring his stew, which was shaved jerky, potatoes, and corn, yet seemed to please everyone.

"One day," Elena said. "How many more?"

"Five or six, with luck."

"Five or six." She let her eyes flicker to Ruff's. "Five days of freedom left."

Justice had forgotten what this journey meant to Elena. A hard, dirty trek across the desert—and at the end of it, an unhappy marriage. There was nothing to say to her, and so he finished his coffee and rose, saying good night.

"Someone coming in."

Ruff turned at the whispered words. Miguel was there in the shadows. His face was drawn. "One of the Jumanos just reported it. A rider coming in."

"One man?" Ruff asked, frowning.

"One man, that is all."

"Maybe someone looking for a meal," Ruff suggested.

"Let us hope so."

It was five minutes more before they heard the clopping of hooves on the backtrail and another minute before the voice called out, "Hello, the camp."

The words were English, the voice heavy with a Mexican accent. Odd, unless someone knew just whose camp this was.

"Come on in, real slow," Justice called back, and in a minute the rider appeared. He sat a tall bay gelding and was dressed in black. A sombrero hung by a string down his back. He wore a huge black mustache.

"All right?" he asked, smiling.

"Come on in. What is it you want?"

He swung down, walking toward Justice, his dark eyes flickering to Miguel; to the Jumanos, who stood to one side, guns in hand; to the fire; and to Elena.

"Just a traveler, hoping to share your fire, sir," he said suavely. "The desert is lonely at night. Lonely and quite dangerous."

Carlos had eased up beside Justice and now he

spoke. "You are welcome to share our fire and our food. Who are you?"

"Just a wanderer named Vargas. That is me. Vargas."

"Where do you work?"

"Ah, *señor*, I am unfortunate in having no employment just now. Perhaps in Sonorita—that is where I am riding now—there is a cousin of mine who has a tannery."

Carlos looked a question at Justice, who could only shrug. Maybe the man was what he said he was, maybe not. At any rate he was no real danger to them alone.

"Sit and eat," Carlos said, and the stranger touched his forehead in a gesture of thanks. He seemed to forget all about them immediately as his eyes lingered on Elena. Lingered long enough to make Carlos uncomfortable.

"Elena, may I speak to you?" he asked, and the woman rose to walk away from the fire, Vargas' obviously admiring eyes following her.

"What's he doing here?"

Pablo was at Ruff's shoulder, his posture belligerent, his eyes smoldering as he studied the newcomer.

"You know him?"

"No. But I know why he's here. Don't you see, he's come to count our guns, to see what our strength is."

"Maybe," Ruff admitted.

Cosacha had ambled up. The Indian was eating stew out of a bowl with his fingers. Some of his food had stuck to his chin.

"Want me to kill him, Ruff Justice?" he asked casually.

"No, of course not. He asked for our hospitality and he's got it."

"I'll find out what he wants," Pablo said, starting forward.

Ruff hooked his arm and hauled the kid back. "You just stay put too, dammit. We'll keep an eye on him, but there's no sense climbing all over the man until we know what he wants."

"He's working for the Trujillos," Pablo answered, jerking his arm from Ruff's grasp.

"I think that is not what makes him want to fight," Cosacha said around a mouthful of food. "I think it is the way this Vargas looks at the woman. As if a man could help looking at such a thing."

Then Cosacha laughed and Ruff saw Pablo stiffen, saw the muscles at the corner of his jaw bunch with anger.

"I think I have touched the nerve," the Indian said, jabbing a food-encrusted finger at Pablo. "The boy wants Elena for himself, eh? But she would not look at a pup like you."

"Damn you!" Pablo started to make a foolish move, and Justice reacted. As the kid went for his gun, Ruff's hand clamped down on his, holding the pistol in his holster. For a minute Pablo fought back wildly, trying to yank the Remington free while Cosacha stood there laughing. Then the kid gave it up. He looked at Justice with pure venom and at Cosacha, who had still not stopped laughing. "One day, Indian," he hissed, "I shall kill you."

Cosacha's eyes went utterly cold. He threw his bowl away and it crashed against the wagon wheel. He started to step in, but Ruff Justice put himself between the two men.

"No, Cosacha. We can't have this. We need every man."

"Tell him then to stay away from me!" Cosacha jabbed that warning finger at Pablo again. "Tell him to go away somewhere and play with his gun."

There was no need for Ruff to tell the kid anything. Pablo spun on his heel and stalked away, still seething with rage. Ruff noticed from the corner of his eye that Vargas had been sitting placidly watching all of this, slowly eating his bowl of stew. He didn't look at all unnerved—in fact, he appeared amused.

"Go on and get some sleep now," Ruff told Cosacha. "We need all the men we have, if it comes to a fight. No sense killing each other."

"No. There is not sense to it," Cosacha said slowly, his eyes still on the shadows where Pablo had disappeared. "But it is a matter of honor, Ruff Justice. The pup will one day be killed. Perhaps by me, perhaps by someone else. For now, I will do as you say. But you tell him to stay away from this Jumano."

Then with an unexpected grin, Cosacha turned and ambled off toward his bed.

Justice, with a last glance at Vargas, decided to do the same.

He untied his bedroll and walked downriver. It was his habit to sleep away from a camp where he could hear better, where he was not so easy to find. Perhaps there was more than one man who wished to find him on this night. Find him and kill him.

Pablo's anger hadn't been directed at Cosacha alone. His flinty eyes had flashed hatred at Ruff Justice as well. Perhaps the reason behind it all was, as Cosacha guessed, Elena. Maybe Pablo saw himself as her lover. Maybe he just wanted to use that damned gun of his on someone, anyone, for any reason.

Ruff spread his roll under the willows and curled up, but sleep didn't come for a long, long while.

There was a whisper of sound, feet passing over the leaf litter, the soft earth. A shadowy movement drew Ruff's eyes. The stars above the willows were clear and bright. The creek muddled past. And Elena came to him.

She was soft and silent, gentle in the night, and Ruff Justice pulled her to him beneath his blanket. When he kissed her, he tasted tears on her face. Her hands were pleading as they tugged at his shirt, reached for his crotch.

"He is so very old," she murmured, "and I am so alone."

Ruff said nothing. His mouth tightened as he

thought about Elena's situation; of the rich man waiting for her, of the end of her youth, the end of her happiness. Then he gave up thinking. She was biting at his neck and he could feel the smear of tears against his throat.

She rose to her knees and unbuttoned her dress, her breasts coming free: young, firm, proud, the dark nipples standing taut. Her waist was very slender. There was a distant light in her eyes as she wriggled free of the dress with a flash of legs, a lithe grace, an urgency.

Ruff slipped out of his pants and pulled his shirt over his head.

Elena was against him again, pressing him down, her breasts flattening against his chest, her mouth open and searching, warm and pliant against his.

Ruff was flat on his back, gazing up at her starlit silhouette. He felt her hand on his hips, then the shift of weight as Elena straddled him, sitting back against his thighs, her head thrown back, her hands tracing circles across his abdomen, then settling on his crotch, finding him ready, rigid.

She lifted him and scooted forward, positioning herself. For a bare fragment of time she was only a focus of warmth, teasing, too near, yet impossibly far away; and then, still holding him, she settled herself, slowly encasing him, slowly bringing the warmth to him.

Ruff's hands reached out and found her breasts. His fingers toyed with her taut nipples, then dropped to join hers between her legs. Their fingers intertwined and Ruff felt the warmth, the delicate moisture, the silky flesh, felt himself entering her, until Elena began to shift and sway, to lift herself ever so slowly, looking as if she would topple over as the blood rushed dizzily through her.

She held herself poised and then buried him in her, hips waggling, buttocks firm and warm against his thighs as she settled.

"Ruff . . ." She fell against him, clutching at him, and her hips began to thrust with purpose, to sway and roll and pitch against him, her pelvis banging his as she built to a furious crescendo.

Ruff clung to her, his hands holding her buttocks, pressing her down against him as she stroked and swayed, her breath coming hotly through her open mouth as she swept his face with her lips and she murmured deep, distant sounds in her throat.

Ruff felt his loins begin to pulse, felt the need rising in him, and she whispered into his ear, urging him on until she went suddenly rigid and with a stifled gasp came completely undone, her body going alternately slack and rigid, her muscles clenching and unclenching, becoming heavy, soft, sweet. Her mouth tore at Ruff's and she lay panting against him, exhausted and dazed.

Ruff held her close in the night, her weight comforting against him, her breath warm and childlike against his chest. Her flesh was cooling and he drew his blanket over them, his hands slowly tracing the contours of her body, the rise of her buttocks, the knuckles of her spine, the smooth shoulders, as night settled and the world went quiet again, the distant chirping of crickets like tiny echoes of their heartbeats.

When he awoke again, she was gone. Slipped from his bed and into the night, leaving only the soft scent of her, the memory. But someone else was there.

Justice came alert instantly, his hand seeking and finding his Colt as he slipped from his bed to move naked into the willows.

A yellow half-moon was rising, casting a net of shadows beneath the willows. It was chill along the river now, and Ruff shivered. Instinct told him there was someone prowling, and his eyes searched the darkness, finding no one.

"Imagination," he grumbled, but it wasn't. He knew somehow—the crickets. He realized then that the crickets had fallen silent, and even in his sleep that had been enough to trigger his survival instincts, the instincts a man who spends much time in wild country develops—or dies.

Ruff held his position, knowing that often he who moves first is he who dies. He never saw the intruder, but the night was suddenly filled with fire and thunder. The gun opened up from out of the brush and Ruff saw his blankets jump, saw five rounds pumped into his bed, the black powder smoke rolling across the clearing as the thunderous echoes blistered the silence of the night.

Then Ruff was on the move, circling toward the unseen attacker, his Colt cocked and ready. From the camp he heard the sounds of activity, men's shouts, boots rushing toward him, and he held up, knowing it was no good now.

The gunman, whoever he was, would have taken to his heels. Moving silently through the brush, Justice was liable to be shot himself, or to have to shoot someone.

He walked back to his bed and slowly dressed as the men from the camp pressed cautiously through the brush. When they entered the clearing, they found Ruff Justice sitting on the ground, his long arms looped around his knees.

He glanced up at them. "What's up, boys?"

"Shots. Someone was shooting," Carlos said.

"Is that what that was?"

"What's going on here?" Pablo asked. The kid looked out of breath. His eyes were lighted with eagerness. Did he want to use that gun—or had he already?

"You saw nothing?" Cosacha asked. The big man's face was unreadable. Was it possible that Cosacha was not as loyal as he pretended to be, that he still held a grudge against Justice for showing him up in front of his men?

"Nothing at all," Ruff answered truthfully. Cosacha's eyes narrowed slightly and Ruff saw what the Jumano had noticed—a bit of Ruff's blanket was smoldering where a bullet had burned it. He patted it out.

"A man who has enemies should not sleep alone," someone said. It was Vargas who spoke. Vargas, who had wandered off the desert to join them, who looked sleek and starched in his tight-fitting vaquero jacket, his dark trousers. And why was he fully dressed at this time of the morning? Just who in hell was he?

"A man with many enemies shouldn't sleep among them," Justice corrected.

"I don't know what in hell's going on here," Carlos said, reverting to his Texas accent under stress, "but I am not having it! Whoever's been potshooting Ruff better slink on out of here while he's still able."

Everyone looked suitably innocent, even Pablo managing it. Justice had risen and was now rolling up his bed. By the stars he guessed it was nearly four-thirty. "May as well roll out now," he said to Carlos. "Everyone's up; the cattle will do better in the coolness."

"All right," Carlos agreed reluctantly. There was enough moon to see by in this country, which was mostly flat, not holding any hidden crevices or coulees to make a night drive impossible. "Cosacha, you want to see to your men? Get those who are on night watch in to eat something. Miguel?"

Miguel did not answer. The old man was simply standing, staring at Ruff Justice. In his hand his pistol still dangled.

"Miguel!"

"*Sí, patrón.*"

"Get the wagon hitched and have Wilfredo get up to the point."

"Yes, *patrón,*" Miguel said stiffly; then the old man, with a last glance at Justice, holstered his gun and slipped off through the brush. Carlos and Ruff Justice were left alone.

"What's happening, Ruff?" the younger man asked.

"I don't know, Carlos, I really don't. I guess it's just

this knack I have for making friends everywhere I go."

"It's not funny, Ruff."

"No," Justice answered, straightening to face Carlos. "It's not funny at all, you're right there. Someone is going to get killed and I don't even know why. I won't know until he tries it again and I take him down. And I will, Carlos, don't let them make any mistake about it. I won't be caught like that again. The next man that fires at me is going to take a load of lead in return. I won't be slack again, because someone damn sure wants me dead."

7

They moved out by moonlight, the cattle bawling and recalcitrant. By the time the sun rose, a fierce yellow ball in the eastern sky, they had settled to the trail and were plodding along across the dry grass desert.

Ruff Justice rode out a way from the herd, his eyes sweeping the land. There was little in the way of feed, little cover. Ironwood grew along a rocky ridge, its wood so hard that the Indians harvested it, not with axes, but with sledgehammers. There was much nopal cactus in the low areas, just now beginning to sprout cactus apples, which were roasted over a fire to burn away the spines, then peeled and eaten. The cactus plants themselves could be similarly converted into decent horse fodder, and the Mexicans made staples and sweet candy from them. There was a low line of chocolate-colored hills to the south, in the direction of Zopilote, and there grew wind-twisted, undernourished cedars and piñon pines.

Ruff halted his horse and wiped his sweatband, watching the cattle amble on, mindless, stupid. Wilfredo was at the point, near him two of the Jumanos. Then the herd with two more Jumanos riding flank on this side, Pablo and another Indian on the far flank. Cosacha rode drag, his scarf up over his face, and beside him Vargas.

Vargas, who should have pulled off that morning, but had pleaded to stay on. There was danger for a man alone, he had said. Well, that was true enough, but Vargas didn't ring true. Not at all.

The wagon came next. Armando sat stiffly in the box, looking like a duck out of water. The butler wasn't cut out for this. Neither was the young, handsome woman sitting beside him, and Ruff let his thoughts linger on Elena for a long while.

Miguel was behind the wagon, alone and silent. The old man was loyal to Carlos, the rancho, the brand. Whatever else he considered was beyond Justice. He was, for the third generation, a loyal honcho, living only for the Trujillos and God help the man who tried to harm Carlos or Rancho Trujillo.

Justice saw the tracks fifteen minutes later and he stepped down from his gray, crouching to examine them. He rose with a slow, breathy curse.

What he had found was the sign of one man afoot. The tracks were very light, but where he had crossed a sandy stretch they were clear. The man had gone to the crest of the knoll and lain flat, looking northward. Toward the herd.

One man afoot.

Justice looked downslope, then back toward the east, seeing nothing yet. But he would. The tracks were of a distinctive nature and any man with the sense of a bean would have been worried by them.

They were Apache. Only the Apache wore those boots, and now somewhere in the shimmering distance there was an Apache who knew that a herd of cattle, a band of wealthy men, men with horses and weapons and plenty of food, was moving through the Apaches' land.

Ruff swung into the saddle, unsheathing his Spencer. He followed the tracks downslope, his face grim. If he saw the Apache scout, he would gun him down without hesitation. Otherwise they would return. They would return and there would be many of them, skilled, merciless fighters.

There were more Apaches in this country than

ever before. Once this desert had been dominated by the Jumanos, Cosacha's people, and by the related Sumas, but Crook had pushed the Apaches into the mountains and across the border, and it was here that these strange, savage nomads—people who had in ages past worked their way down from Canada, terrorizing and destroying as they went—would make their last stand.

Ruff halted the horse. The tracks had vanished in a rocky feeder arroyo and he had been able to pick up the sign again. He spent another hour, casting this way and that among the rocks the color of smoke, the mesquite and cholla, but he was unable to pick up the scout's sign.

He turned the gray then and rode back to the herd, finding Carlos now on the left flank.

"Trouble," Justice said.

"Dunweather? The Trujillos?"

"Worse. Apaches. We've been spotted and they'll come back, Carlos. We've got a lot of meat on the hoof here, a lot of valuable weapons."

"Damn." Carlos sighed. He removed his wide-brimmed dark hat and mopped his forehead. "What's to be done?"

"Nothing. Just nothing at all," Justice had to tell him. "Stay alert, keep your weapons to hand."

Carlos nodded. He looked pale beneath his tan and the coat of sweat-streaked dust on his face. "All right," he answered, "I'll pass the word. Is there any point in sending out more lookouts?"

"No, I don't think so. You'll just weaken yourself by spreading your men out. Besides," he said with a wry smile, "we'll never see them until they want us to."

Justice had fought the Apache too many times not to be worried. The Apache could find concealment behind a blade of grass. It was nothing for a band of Apaches to bury themselves in the sand and lie immobile for hours waiting for their enemy to approach them and then rise up out of the ground like earth demons.

There has never been a better fighting man on this earth. If they wanted the herd, they would come, and Ruff could only rely on superior weaponry.

Justice rode past the wagon, and Elena's eyes widened. She started to speak but closed her mouth again, her eyes moist and shining.

"There may be some Indians about, Armando," Ruff told the driver, deliberately downplaying the danger. "If anything starts up, just halt the wagon—you'll not outrun them anyway. We'll be back to help out."

"Yes. Ruff Justice," the butler said. He looked weary and overheated. Justice looked at Elena, offered her what he hoped was a comforting smile, and turned the gray away.

"I smell them."

Cosacha was beside Ruff, his ugly face set and dark. "I smell Apache, Justice."

"You're right, I saw their sign over the sandhills."

"Stinking Apache," Cosacha mumbled. "They are animals. Once when I was a boy they came to our camp. The women they mutilated. The children, their heads dashed against rocks. Part of my family too, you understand, Justice?"

"I understand."

"Very proud warrior, very admired. You know what they are? Cowards who sneak through the shadows, who hide and kill. They will not stand up to you unless there are many of them and you are few."

Maybe, although Ruff's experience hadn't supported that point of view. Cosacha was speaking from deep, soulful bitterness, a blood hatred was at work here, a racial antipathy.

"What should we do?" he asked with a heavy sigh, his ranting over.

"Stay alert. If there's trouble, forget the cattle. Let

them run, we won't be able to stop them anyway. Group at the wagon. I won't let them have the woman."

"I think maybe you like her," Cosacha said slyly.

"Show me a man who wouldn't," Justice answered flippantly.

"Who was it last night, Justice?" the Jumano asked.

"I don't know what you mean."

"Someone came to kill you. Was it over the woman? Was it the pup, this Pablo?"

"I don't know, Cosacha. Who was it?" Ruff was looking intently at the Indian as they rode side by side toward the point of the lumbering herd.

"What are you asking me?" Cosacha asked darkly. "Was it you?"

"Me!" Cosacha went rigid. He reined in his horse roughly. His hands were clenched into fists, the tendons on his neck stood out like cables. Then he threw back his head and laughed, roared with laughter. "No, Justice, not me. Why do I kill you?"

"I thought it was possible you were still mad about the fight. That you wanted to prove something."

"Not me," Cosacha said soberly. "Not me, kill like a stinking Apache from the darkness. No, Justice, if ever Cosacha wishes to kill, you will know it. You will see his face and hear the words from his own lips."

And Justice believed him. He nodded and said, "Tell your men about the Apaches."

"I will, but they know already, Justice. I have told you—a Jumano can smell them. And a Jumano—he hopes that the dogs of the desert are foolish enough to attack."

Justice had no such hope. His only hope was that the Apaches were members of a small band, that the numbers of armed men they had seen would deter them from attacking the herd.

It was a feeble hope.

Justice rode out wide to the south once again, his eyes squinting into the desert sun, probing for any movement out on the land, which stretched away to the ends of the earth, hiding behind shimmering veils of rising heat.

He was irritable and physically uncomfortable. His shirt clung to his back, his hands and neck were sunburned and raw. A dull headache had developed behind his left eye. Justice halted his horse and stepped down on the rocky rise to douse himself with water from his canteen.

When the shots came, they were not unexpected, yet they jarred against Ruff's anticipations. Something was wrong. There were three shots, evenly spaced, and then no more.

He was aboard the gray in seconds, riding flat out toward the point of the herd. He could see some sort of activity up ahead but could not make it out.

He looked right and left, seeing no signs of battle, hearing no shouts, no rifle reports. Elena was standing in the wagon box, looking at him expectantly, fearful. Miguel, on the far side of the milling herd, was riding apace toward the point.

They were already too late. By the time the fourth shot sounded, it was over.

Carlos stood before the Apache. He had appeared out of nowhere to stand before the herd, arms folded, a rifle in his right hand.

Carlos lifted a hand, signaling to his men to slow the herd, but it was too late for that. The cattle separated, forking around the bronzed Apache warrior, streaming up the trail, which ran between two dung-colored, grassless hills.

"What is it?" Pablo was breathless. His hat had blown back off his head and now hung by its string. His hair was in his eyes.

"I don't know." Carlos looked around for Justice, for Miguel, but both men were far behind them. Carlos' horse backed in a tight cirle, nervous and wild-eyed. He settled the horse and pushed through a gap in the cattle to halt beside the Indian, Pablo at his shoulder.

"*Buenos días*," the Apache said in a cultivated, mission-school Spanish.

"What do you want?" Pablo demanded heatedly.

"I am Three Toes, a Chiricahua." The Apache did not move, except to unfold his arms. The cattle had slowed now and been pushed to the north so that they no longer forked the Apache and his inquisitors.

"What do you want?" Carlos asked again.

"It is a simple matter," the Apache said. "You have much beef. My tribe has little. You are passing through our land. For that privilege you should pay."

"Be damned!" Pablo exploded. "Don't stand for this piracy, Señor Trujillo."

"Wait a minute, calm down. Dammit, where's Justice?" Carlos turned again to Three Toes, leaning across the withers of his horse to study the Apache's grave face. "How many head do you want to pass through."

"Fifteen."

"Señor Trujillo!" Pablo shouted, angrily leaping down from his horse to walk to Carlos and look up at him with those obsidian eyes. "You can't pay this man anything. If you do, every damned Apache between here and the border will come along asking for the same."

"Fifteen cows," the Apache said casually. "And you may travel as you please. We are not eager for war. The signs are bad."

"That means there aren't many of them," Pablo said triumphantly, wheeling toward the Indian. "Get the hell out of here," he ordered.

"If you wish to . . ." Then it happened. The Apache brought his hands up, perhaps to recross his arms, perhaps he actually was going to fire his weapon as Pablo in that critical half-second believed.

It didn't matter what the Apache's intentions were a moment later. Pablo, going to a knee, drew his Rem-

ington revolver and fired once. The bullet caught
the Apache in the face, creating a third bloody eye
where the nose had been. The back of the Indian's
head was blown away like an exploded melon and he
was thrown back to sprawl against the sand, dead.

Ruff Justice, coming on the run, saw the Indian
blown back, saw Carlos throw up a hand in despair,
saw Pablo walk toward the Indian, his shoulders
rolling in an exaggerated swagger.

Justice leaped from the gray's back and caught the
kid in midair. They went down in a heap, Pablo's gun
flying free as Justice crashed into him.

They landed hard, startling the nearby cattle. Pablo
swore and grunted with pain. Justice turned him
over and yanked his head up, slapping him hard
across the face three times. Then he stepped back,
long hair in his eyes, his hand on his holstered Colt.

"Now you can have it, damn you! Get up and get
your gun, Pablo. You hear me, do it!"

"Ruff . . ." Carlos murmured.

"Stay out of it, Carlos. He killed that Apache cold.
Do you know what we've got now? We've got us a
war with his tribe. All because Junior just had to use
his pretty gun. Now he can use it again—on me. Pick
it up, Pablo!"

Pablo made no move. He sat against the earth,
staring at the tall man hovering over him. Pablo
hadn't seen eyes like those before, eyes that had seen
death and would see it again, cold blue eyes that at
this moment were utterly without expression, but
alert as a big cat's.

Miguel had arrived, and Wilfredo. Pablo's eyes
flickered to them and then back to the tall man who
was waiting, waiting.

"Well," Justice said, his mouth twisting into a bitter
expression, "let's do it, pup. Pick it up. See how you
like facing a man who's fighting back."

Pablo's hand stretched out and hung wavering over

his pistol. He tried to will his fingers to work, to pick it up, but they would not obey his mental commands.

"Mr. Ruff Justice," Wilfredo said, "he is my son. I beg you."

"Let it go, Ruff, please," Carlos said.

It was a long minute before Justice cooled, then he nodded. He walked to Pablo, leaned over, and picked up the kid's pistol. He winged it into the brush beside the road. Pablo didn't move. He didn't move as Justice walked to Pablo's horse and removed the Winchester from his saddle boot, jacked all the shells out of it, and heaved it into the brush as well.

"Get on your horse and get out of here," Justice said quietly. He didn't even look at Pablo. He was looking into the distance, studying the pale sky, the clouds that were beginning to gather to the north. "Get going and keep going."

Pablo started to speak, clamped his jaw shut, and rose, dusting himself. He planted his hat and walked to his horse, swinging a leg over. Then with a last glance at his father, who stood, head bowed, by Justice, he yanked his horse's head around and slapped the spurs to it.

In another minute he was gone, leaving only a slowly settling cloud of dust. And a dead Apache warrior.

"What do we do now?" Carlos asked.

"Bury him. Then push these cattle until their hooves are worn off. That's all we can do," Ruff told him, "but it won't be enough."

The Apaches did not come that day, nor the next. The herd pushed onward, striking across the harsh desert. There was almost no graze now, little water, and the weaker of the herd began to drop. The heat, which had been moderate, grew intense. They rode stultified beneath the harsh white sun, choking on gritty dust, their vision distorted by the rising waves of heat. For two nights running the cattle had bed-

ded down without water or grass, and they were
wild-eyed, bawling constantly.

They pushed the herd to their limit, but it was not
fast enough if the Apaches chose to pursue. The
border was impossibly distant across miles of white-
sand desert, over broken rocky hills. Tempers grew
short. Salt sweat clung to everyone. The miles, the
hours seemed to gain them nothing.

"We will not make it," Wilfredo said. His eyes were
red-rimmed, watery. "It is too far."

"If we can make the Pecos, we will be all right,"
Carlos said. He sat mopping his throat and face with
his scarf. The dry wind kicked up sand and tugged
at their clothing. To the north and west the thunderheads they had seen for the last few days continued
to build, threatening rain that never fell, that left
them parched and leathery.

"There is water in Chichachero," Miguel said. The
old man looked much the same as the day they left
Rancho Trujillo, as if he had seen so many suns, so
many miles of desert that it no longer had any effect
on him.

"Chichachero?"

"In the hills," Miguel said, inclining his head. "There
is always water there from a spring."

"Ruff?"

"We need to water these cows soon or lose them,"
Justice answered.

"But you don't like it?"

"No. I don't like anything that takes us farther
west. Chato Chavez."

Carlos sucked in his breath at the mention of the
bandit's name. "He is nearby?"

"No one seems to know, and I for one don't want
to find out. I'd almost prefer the Apaches."

"And I," Miguel said quietly. "Still, Mr. Ruff Justice,
we will never reach the Pecos with this herd. You
passed over the land on your way south. You saw

what water there is. Enough for a man and his single horse, but not for a herd of steers."

"I'd vote for the Chichachero," Vargas said. He smiled. "If I had a vote, that is."

"You don't," Carlos said.

The man stuck with them, working cattle, eating their food. Probably they should have thrown him out, but there was no real cause to do so. He was an extra hand, an extra gun, and the desert was alive with Apaches.

"That's a little out of the way if you're heading for your cousin's in Sonorita, isn't it?" Justice asked.

For just a moment Vargas' eyes flashed with unreadable emotion, then that spark died and Vargas said smoothly, "I am with the herd now. I think that what is best for the herd is best for me. My cousin is in no hurry to see me, nor I to see him."

It was a good-enough answer, but Justice didn't find it particularly convincing. He glanced at Carlos, who looked worn-down, exhausted.

"What do you want to do, Carlos?"

"If we do not water them soon, we will have no herd. Without the herd the journey is pointless."

"All right." Ruff rose. "Chichachero, then."

"If those clouds would move in, we wouldn't have to worry about water," Wilfredo said. He stood looking to the north, where the gray, anvil-headed clouds hung motionless in the sky. Each morning they loomed up off the horizon and hung menacingly in the sky, only to draw back and wither at dusk.

"Well," Justice said, "we can't wait on their whim. West then, to Chichachero." And, he thought, God help us if Chavez is holed up in those hills.

8

Night brought no relief from the heat. They lay in their beds bludgeoned by exhaustion, sweat trickling off their bodies. In the distance thunder rumbled ominously and an occasional flash of lightning arced across the skies, too far distant to stampede the cattle, yet not far enough way to prevent them from growing more and more edgy.

No one ate anymore. Not at breakfast time, when the men drank down as many cups of coffee as they could hold, knowing it would sweat off in an hour or two, needing it to pummel numbed senses into some semblance of alertness.

Justice saddled his gray and slipped the bit into its reluctant mouth. The hour was early as he led his horse toward the fire. The Jumanos sat in a silent cluster, eyes glancing his way as he walked to the wagon where Elena stood holding an untouched plate of beef and rice in her hands.

"Who can eat?" She sighed.

"No one, apparently. Except Cosacha. He'll eat anything that gets in his way and lies still long enough."

"We are turning away from the border," the woman said.

"That's right."

"I thought so. I am not so good at directions, but even I notice where the sun comes up. Why are we doing this, Ruff?"

"We need water badly. Miguel knows of a place off to the west."

I thought—" She smiled weakly and looked to the north. "I thought we wanted to strike out northward as quickly as possible. The Apaches . . ."

"Maybe they won't come," Ruff said, touching her hair. She leaned her head against his palm briefly. "If they didn't find the dead man, they might not."

"You are telling me fairy tales, Ruff Justice," Elena said, and Justice laughed.

"Yes," he admitted, "I am. But as has been pointed out to me, if we reach the border without the cattle, this has all been pointless, a waste of time."

"I see . . ." Elena nodded thoughtfully.

"Of course, if you are in a hurry to get north . . ."

"That is not funny, Ruffin T. Justice." She got onto tiptoes after looking around and kissed him gently, quickly.

"No, it's not. I'm sorry."

"Make it up to me," she said, her lips parting, her eyes searching his.

"Here?" He laughed.

"Anywhere," she said breathily.

Justice noticed that they were being watched and he stepped back. It was only Miguel, whose face was expressionless, whose eyes said nothing.

"Elena"—Ruff leaned against the wagon wheel, removing his hat to wipe back his dark hair—"isn't there some other way out for you? Lord, woman, I hate to think of you chained to a man you care nothing about."

"You are asking me to marry you?" she asked with an impish smile.

"You know I'm not," Ruff told her soberly, and she seemed to shrink a little. "But there must be another way. Why marry this William Dobbs at all? You can do other things."

"Live in poverty?" she asked, straightening up, her eyes proud, haughty. "Or dance in a saloon? No, I will not do this. There is a need for me, for my body,

Ruff Justice. My people have only me to rely on. An honorable marriage will provide for us."

There was power and determination in her voice, and for one of the few times in his life Justice found himself wishing he were a wealthy man. She deserved to live as she wanted, to be independent and happy.

Armando had begun to hitch the team now and Elena, climbing aboard the wagon, sat her bench, hands folded, looking out upon the desert as dawn broke, spattering the land and the hesitant high clouds with fire and gold.

Justice led out, hearing the shouts of the drovers behind him, the mournful bawling of the steers as they were forced into motion once again.

The hills rose sharply before them now, jagged, barren, dark brown. There was no life there at all, it seemed, but the barrel cactus, the yucca. Yet deeper in the hills, Miguel insisted, there was a spring rising from deep in the earth, and around it grass and palm trees.

Ruff glanced again to the north, seeing the same iron-gray thunderheads that hung there like watchdogs each day. The sun rose higher, a flaming red ball, branding faces and hands, all exposed flesh. The wind began to build, whistling through the rocky hills, drifting sand and light debris.

They rode on through the day, the cattle hanging their heads, tongues dangling. Justice squinted into the white light, the furnace like heat of the day. Still they saw nothing green, still the weary cattle did not smell water.

It was not until sundown, when the hills rising up three or four hundred feet beside the trail began to go purple with the dusky light, that Ruff's horse pricked up its ears and flared its nostrils and began of its own volition to move ahead at a quicker, almost-eager pace.

"Hold them back!" Ruff called across his shoulder.

For the cattle too had begun to come alert, smelling water, and in another minute Ruff recognized that the herd could not be held back. Swinging the gray to one side, he watched as the steers, spurred on by the enticing scent, rumbled forward, lurching into motion as one giant, many-legged beast, and pressed through the pass toward their goal.

"Let them go," Carlos was shouting, "let them go." And the herders pulled off, letting the cattle have their head. In the dust that sifted down in their wake, Ruff Justice entered the hidden canyon of Chichachero.

At that moment it was the most beautiful place on earth. The sundown skies had gone to a deep orange, and standing in sharp relief against the sky were tall palm trees appearing black and fanciful. There was a broad, silver disc on the floor of the canyon, and there the cattle had gathered. Water. The spring still flowed and the cattle, dehydrated, exhausted, clustered at the edge of the pond, lowing and shouldering each other aside.

Ruff, grinning with relief, rode his gray forward, guiding it to the far side of the pool, where he let it drink, dipping its muzzle into the deep silver lake, tossing its head with delighted surprise as it tasted clear, cold water.

"Made it." Carlos was beside Ruff, climbing shakily down from his roan. He watched his herd drink, relief easing the hard mask his face had formed itself into these last days.

Beyond the pool was a grove of palms. Higher up other trees clung to the rocks tenaciously. The wind was muted, blunted by the walls of the canyon.

"A bit of paradise, isn't it?" the young man asked.

"It is that, Carlos, it is that." It was salvation for the herd. In a day or so they would be plump with water, ready to attempt the last leg of the trek, their hooves healed, their spirits raised.

"Have you been seeing Elena?" Carlos asked out

of the blue. He was looking away from Justice. He stood holding his horse's reins loosely, staring at the orange and velvet of the late sky.

"Yes," Ruff answered, "I have."

"That's what I thought."

"Does it bother you, Carlos?"

"Yes, Ruff, it does. It bothers me. I don't know why it should, but it does."

Silence descended with the night, and when Ruff figured the gray had had enough water, he led it away some distance to where grass grew between the palms and he hobbled it, leaving it to graze contentedly.

A red cone of fire marked the campsite and Ruff walked toward it, his rifle over his shoulder. He found Cosacha first.

"You have someone posted at the mouth of the canyon?"

"Two men," the Jumano said. "But if the Apaches come . . ."

"If they come, we'll deal with it as best we can."

"It is bad to remain here for long," Cosacha said. He had a point. The longer they remained in any one spot, the greater the chances that the Apaches would catch up with them.

"Nothing to do about that," Justice had to tell him. "We can't carry those steers north. They're played out."

In the darkness Justice couldn't see the big Indian's expression.

"Well," Cosacha said at length, "it is a few extra days, a few extra dollars for us."

And that, Ruff Justice considered, was about all you could say for their situation. They had found a little island of comfort in the desert vastness, a small paradise, but outside the canyon walls, death still lurked, and it was creeping nearer with each passing hour.

There was a second higher pool among the jumbled rocks, and from that they filled their water barrels and canteens. When that task was done, it was full dark, and Justice sat perched alone in the rocks, staring down at the firelit camp.

Carlos hadn't been very happy about things where Elena was concerned. He had said that there was nothing between himself and Elena when Justice had asked him. Perhaps that wasn't the same as Carlos saying he didn't wish there was something between them. Would Carlos work himself up enough to empty a revolver into Ruff's bed? Ruff didn't think so, he didn't want to believe it was Carlos Trujillo who had tried to kill him.

"You just never knew where a woman was concerned. It could be that Carlos had gone haywire. As Pablo apparently had.

Ruff stood and looked toward the mouth of the canyon, at the starlit desert beyond. Then, feeling gritty, weary, he stripped off his buckskins and eased into the pool.

It sat seventy feet up the hill on a shelf where water trickling down from the spring had carved a stony basin over the centuries. The water was dark and icy, the air still warm. Ranks of fan palms crowded the edge of the pool, rustling fronds clattering in the breeze. Above, the rounded peaks of the rocky hills blacked out the hem of the starlit sky. The moon was a pale promise against the eastern sky.

A horse whickered below, across the camp. The fire wavered in the breeze. Ruff sunk beneath the water, the coldness probing to the bone, invigorating him. He swam to the far side of the pond, some fifty feet away, and clambered out beneath the palms.

The wind whipping across his body was chilling and he dived in again, swimming in a frog stroke back toward his clothes. Emerging, he shook his head to clear the long dark hair from his eyes, turned, and dived back in, feeling totally alert now. A warm meal and a good night's sleep, and he would be ready for the trail again.

He reached the far side, stretched out a hand, and pulled himself out of the water—and halted dead, crouching in the black pools of the shadow beneath the palms.

There was someone moving around the pond's edge and now by starlight he saw his clothing being picked up, examined, and thrown over an arm. Then the person picked up Ruff's gunbelt and Spencer.

The man stopped, rifle in hand, staring across the pond, but there was no movement to call his eyes to where Justice crouched, motionless, his teeth chattering with the cold. There was no sound, nothing but the whisper of the wind through the palms, and the man with the rifle turned, taking Ruff's buckskins with him. The buckskins and his weapons.

Why Justice hadn't called out, he wasn't sure. Some instinct had warned him against it. It wasn't that the man with the rifle was unfamiliar—at that distance, in that light, he could have been anyone from President Hayes to Adam. But Justice did not move, did not call out, and a moment later the gunfire erupted.

The horrible scream of pain seemed to come first, then the roar of a big-bored rifle. Then there was a chain of gunfire, like a string of firecrackers going off in the camp below.

Justice could see muzzle flashes on the hillslope opposite, hear a wounded horse whinny shrilly, the cattle rise to their feet in a muffled rumbling.

Then he was circling through the palms, tearing bare feet on rocks, his naked body filmed with moisture, his hair hanging limply, his eyes alert, searching.

He nearly ran into the man with the Winchester. The man's head came around as Ruff, bursting from the trees, caught sight of him. The Winchester started to come up, but Justice was already to him, mauling him like a panther. His knee went to the man's groin, stiffened fingers struck out at his eyes. When he raised his arms to try to protect his face, Justice hammered a fist to his wind.

He doubled up and Justice tore the rifle from his grip, wielding it like a club. The stock came down with enough force to split his skull. Justice heard bone crack—or maybe it was the stock itself. The man went down with a groan and Justice stood over him for a moment, reversing the rifle, holding it ready.

But he lay still on the ground. No one else seemed to be around. The rifle fire from below had stopped as abruptly as it had begun and there was only the wind howling down the canyon, the rumble of milling cattle.

Justice crouched down, examining the man on the ground.

He wasn't dead, but he might well be on his way out. At the least he would have a headache for a month or so. He was Mexican, tall, broad-shouldered, wearing clothing that hadn't been washed for a while.

Justice began yanking his boots off.

In minutes he was dressed in a shirt that was too big at the shoulders and chest, one that hadn't been in hailing distance of soap since it was made; the pants were long as well, heavy twill, with a hole in the knee. The sombrero fit. The boots were much too big.

Justice moved out, creeping around the edge of the pool, keeping to the rocks. The moon had risen higher, and the pond and all around it was illuminated as if by beacons.

Justice still could not see the camp below. He could make out voices from time to time, speaking Spanish. He remained crouched in the shadows for another five minutes before he began working his way toward the edge of the bluff.

His boots! Somehow they had been left behind and Justice made for them. It was as if he had found the mother lode. He didn't care much what was on his back, except for the smell, but he wouldn't make it far in those oversized clodhoppers he had taken from the Mexican.

He tugged them on, finding his skinning knife in place—six inches of razor steel designed for fleshing out hides, sharp enough to split a hair three ways—it wasn't of much use just now. Nor was the rifle.

He crawled to the edge of the bluff and looked down into the camp. The fire was glowing softly. Two still figures lay against the earth. One of them was Wilfredo, the other a Jumano.

Near the fire another man sat, his legs stretched out in that peculiar braced posture of someone badly wounded. He thought it was Armando, but couldn't be sure. If it was, the butler wouldn't be around much longer. He had a horrible scarlet smear across his shirtfront. His head lolled on his neck as if there was no muscle there to hold it up.

The big man stood near the fire, hands on hips. Silver needlework decorated his pantlegs and the band of his sombrero. Around him stood a dozen armed men, and on their knees before him were Carlos, Vargas, and Miguel. Cosacha lay clubbed to the earth nearby. And facing the man was Elena María Cortes, her chin held high, her arms folded, her hair unpinned and firelit, her mouth proud.

Ruff heard the man laugh, saw him stretch out a hand toward Elena, and he swore that if he molested her he would shoot him, whatever followed be damned.

The hand rested on Elena's shoulder and she slapped it away. "Pig," he heard her spit, and the man laughed. But he left her alone, turning to give rapid instructions to his men.

"Get the cattle up to the hole. Tonight we shall eat, *compadres*. There will be beef to last us until the Federales have run themselves blind on the desert. Fernando, drag the dead into the rocks. Then bring the wagon along—and the woman with you."

"*Sí,* Chato," the man replied, confirming what Justice had already suspected, already feared. The man in the silver-embroidered clothes was Chato Chavez, cutthroat, enemy of the people, bandit, killer.

Ruff settled in, watching the activity below. Chavez must have had at least thirty men with him, and they got to work efficiently. The cattle were already being herded toward the mouth of the canyon. Elena was being helped into the wagon and Ruff saw her shake off the helping hand of a man who laughed loudly at her fiery independence.

Carlos also rode in the wagon. He was holding an arm as if it were broken. Miguel followed them in, the old man stiff and unbending. Cosacha was thrown in without ceremony.

And then the wagon was driven out, flanked by six riders. In minutes the canyon was empty, silent. There was only the whispering wind, the slowly settling dust, and Ruff Justice alone and on foot in the middle of the endless desert.

Ruff waited another half-hour before he went down to the camp. He examined the bodies by moonlight: Wilfredo, Armando, two of Cosacha's Jumanos, and an unknown man, one of Chavez' riders undoubtedly.

He looked around once more and then started walking. He had no water, no food, no horse—they had taken the gray—and only the ammunition that was in the borrowed rifle, but he started forward, following the tracks of the herd.

They had the army beef, they had his clothes and his horse. All right, they could have all of that and be damned—but they couldn't have the black-eyed beauty Elena Cortes. That was more in the nature of personal property, and if Chavez thought he had trouble with half of the Mexican army on his tail, he would find out there could be much worse things. Justice was coming.

He jogged on through the night, running across

the broken ground to the west of the canyon, the hills looming over him, the pale moon at his back.

Nothing moved out on the desert flats but the lean man in the ill-fitting clothes, and the wind. There was no sound but the whisper of his boots over sand and the occasional distant howl of a mournful coyote.

With the dawn he was still running. The sand pinkened and then went to a brilliant white. The sun battered at him, searing him between the shoulder blades. He was into the hills by midmorning, still jogging, his breath coming in rasping gasps, his feet swollen and fiery.

When he could run no more, he dragged himself up into the rocks, his heart hammering in his chest, his eyes puffy and red, his legs wobbly, and he fell to sleep in the terrible midday heat, propped up against a mammoth brown boulder, rifle across his knees.

Dusk brought him to life again. He rose stiffly, his tongue cleaving to his palate, his joints grating, eyes rimmed with secretion. His head throbbed dully as he rose to survey the land below and ahead of him.

The trail wound into the rocky hills that stretched out for miles to the west and south. It was a devil's playground, a sea of rocks and knobby hills. Undoubtedly there were lookouts posted on the key hills, alert for the approach of the Mexican army.

One man, Ruff considered, had a chance of slipping through them. "Just what in hell," he asked himself, "does he do after he's gotten in?"

He wasn't going to take them all down, not with the six bullets in the Winchester rifle he carried, and he wasn't going to smuggle Carlos and Elena back out.

There was no real choice, and so he started on. There was nowhere else to go afoot in that country. Anyplace he could go for help was too distant, the odds against reaching it minimal. And so he went ahead, not thinking about the danger ahead, but only of his next step, and his next.

Justice couldn't afford to chance using the trail, and so he jogged over the rough ground beside it. Down washes and up cactus-clogged arroyos, over masses of volcanic boulders, the shaggy Joshua trees standing black and gaunt against the moonlit sky.

He went down twice, three times, a dozen times in those moon-shadowed hills, once cracking his knee hard enough to temporarily paralyze that leg. Justice sat there cursing, his lip curled back with pain, holding the knee, his head bowed.

He heard the horses then and his head came up sharply. Forgetting the pain in his knee, he ran toward the road stiff-legged, his head bobbing. He slipped and slid down a sandy chute to the bottom of the gorge, where it was cool and damp. Something was startled away in the nearby brush, something large by the sound it made as Justice legged it toward the road.

He scrambled up a shale-littered incline, ducking beneath the outstretched, thorny arms of a tangle of mesquite to emerge on a shelf above the trail.

Just then they came around the bend in the road— two men riding side by side down the dark trail, their horses keeping an easy pace.

Glancing to the right, Justice noticed that the trail narrowed as it passed between two upthrust boulders, and he considered matters. They had horses and he wanted them. They undoubtedly had guns and ammunition. He wanted those. And they must have water—just then he thought he would gladly kill for a drink of water.

But the attempt would have to be silent. Shots fired might bring help pouring down that road. Shots fired into Ruff's body would bring an unhappy end to the experiment.

He took no more than a fraction of a second to consider all of that and then he was off again, climbing down the ledge into the gorge, scrambling across that and clambering up the dark bulk of the ancient, seamed boulder.

Panting, he reached the crest and crawled out onto it. He was none too soon. The riders weren't a hundred feet away and Ruff crouched, ready and alert, his muscles coiled, his eyes lit with animal intensity. He kept the Winchester in hand, although he had no intention of firing it unless necessary—it might damned well become necessary.

He held it in his left hand and filled his right hand with the deadly steel of his skinning knife. As the horses neared, he crouched lower yet and then, timing his leap, vaulted into space.

He hit the first rider flush, slamming him into the second. Both men tumbled to the ground, the horses rearing and pawing at the air. Ruff had his knife to the bandit's throat, and even as they both fell, he yanked back and to the right, slitting the trachea, opening the jugular. Blood spilled across his hands and the thrashing outlaw convulsed, dying in Ruff's arms.

He dropped the bandit and turned to face the second, an enormous Mexican with a shaggy black beard. He had lost his rifle in his fall, but now he spotted it.

The bandit dived and Justice was after him. Too slowly.

The big man turned, bringing his rifle to his shoulder, and Ruff, exposed, took his only chance. The skinning knife tumbled through the air, performing a revolution and a half before burying itself in the outlaw's throat just above the collarbone.

Gagging, he staggered back, dropping the rifle, both hands clutching at the knife. He never did manage to get it out. With a last gurgling sound, a wild wave of his hand, he toppled forward, to lie dying on the hard earth.

Justice was to him in a second, yanking the knife free, his eyes flickering to the backtrail. He heard no

more approaching horses, however, and proceeded
to strip the bodies of weapons.

Then he dragged them to the rocky drop-off on
the far side of the trail and rolled them over, watching
them jolt to a stop in the deep ravine. A thorough
search would find them quickly, but a casual glance
from the trail would not discover the bodies.

Ruff saw one of the horses, a deep-chested bay
standing watching apprehensively. The other had
kept running.

"Easy, boy, here you are." Justice kept his voice
low and soothing, and on the second try he managed
to catch the reins to the bay.

The second horse took a little more doing. It had
taken to the brush and it took Justice half an hour of
working it before he managed to corner the animal.
Still he couldn't afford to have let that animal go.
Likely it would have made its way back to camp,
riderless, blood on the saddle.

It was a leggy blue roan with a black mane and
tail, wild-eyed and frightened. Ruff managed to soothe
it some. Then he led both horses farther from the
trail, hobbled them, and got to examining his booty.

The water first. He took the canteen from the
roan's saddle and drank deeply, pouring it over his
face, rubbing his eyes free of grit, soaking his hair.
Then he sat and carefully washed his feet, finding a
few blisters, one the size of a silver dollar.

The belt guns he kept, using one holster, the other
pistol shoved behind his belt. Both were in excellent
condition, apparently worked over by a master gun-
smith and kept cleaned and oiled. They were a
bandit's tools of trade, and if a cowboy might leave a
gun in his holster in all weather until it rusted, an
outlaw was always meticulous in the care of his
weapons—and in the choice of horseflesh. Both animals before Ruff were prime stock, long-runners
kept grained and curried.

He kept one rifle, the .44 Henry. The other was

one of the new .30-caliber Winchesters, and that one he tossed into the brush.

Then he sat down to a meal. Jerky, hardtack, and water, plenty of water. The bandits had been carrying a quantity of food, leading Justice to believe they were making a long journey somewhere. But where? There was no answer to be found on the bodies of the bandits, none in their saddlebags.

Finished with his hasty, filling meal, Ruff rose and stretched his long arms, glancing at the high-riding moon.

Then he walked to the horses again. Slipping the lariat from the saddle of the bay, he looped the startled roan's neck and led off up the long canyons.

Ruff felt no fear just then, only a certain edginess. He decided it was a form of madness, this sense of calm deliberation that came over him at times like this. He hadn't a hope in hell of getting Elena and Carlos out of there. Hadn't much hope of surviving himself.

Yet, having made his decision to attempt it, he had placed fear aside and was concentrating only on how best to achieve what he had put his mind to.

"If you'd ever put your mind to anything worth a damn, Mr. Ruffin T. Justice, you'd show them something," he muttered to the horse, which pricked its ears, wondering at this new master.

The wind had begun to build again, chilling Ruff as he rode higher into the ancient hills. Glancing back, he saw that at long last those thunderheads were drifting in—and there couldn't have been a worse time for it.

In another hour they had bulged up until the moon was covered and the land went dark. Ruff had to slow to a crawl. The going was rough; it was easy country for a horse to break a leg in.

He crested a line of jumbled hills where wind-gnarled cedar clung to the shallow soil, their roots clinging desperately to the rocks surrounding them.

Thunder rumbled behind him and the skies flared briefly with distant lightning.

Ruff scanned the land spread out below him. Most of it was lost in impenetrable shadow now, only the high ridges stark against the skyline clearly defined. But, dammit, somewhere down there was a bandit camp; somewhere the woman slept this night—or lay awake, staring at the sky, her heart convulsing.

He had started down off the ridge already when he saw it. Ruff yanked back the reins hard enough to startle the bay. Then he backed the horse a little.

There hadn't been much, but it had been enough to catch his eye against the prevailing blackness of the land. Now he saw it again, glowing dimly through what must have been a notch in the string of saddlebacks opposite his position.

Fire.

A dim reddish glow winking at him across the miles, and there could be only one camp in these hills—Chato Chavez would tolerate no neighbors.

Ruff started off again, his mouth set grimly, his eyes on the landmarks he had picked out to guide him to the distant fire. His mouth was dry, his muscles bunched uncomfortably, yet there was a strange elation in his heart. He would have his try, and win or lose, Chato Chavez would discover that there were other dogs with teeth.

It was another two hours before he reached the camp he had seen from the ridge. By that time the skies had opened up and with a blustering rush of wind the rain had fallen.

Lightning scored the dark sky; and thunder, like the cannon of opposing armies, bellowed, the sound echoing up the long canyons.

Justice hunched his shoulders and rode on, the wind tearing at his hair, his flesh, with icy fingers. The rain came down in sheets and he was soaked to the bone in half an hour. The bay beneath him plodded on. The ground was dark and murky, silver sheets of water running off the hills.

There was no fire now to guide him and he could pick out his landmarks only at intervals, when the low-hanging clouds parted as the wind tore gaps in their ranks.

He could see nothing, but neither, he hoped, could anyone see him approaching the camp. He paused on a low knoll, peering downslope toward the trail, which after winding far away from him had found its way back. Beyond the next low line of hills, he thought.

Lightning flashed near enough for Justice to taste the sulfurous smell of it. On its heels came a clap of thunder loud enough to rattle his eardrums. The horse shied wildly and Ruff had to tight-rein him and settle the bay.

Lightning flickered across the sky again, like a white darting snake's tongue, and Ruff Justice smiled slowly. By the light of the storm he had seen it. The camp was set in a high valley with rising peaks like battlements surrounding it.

He hadn't seen much detail, but he had made out three or four cabins, apparently of stone, a milling cattle herd, and a wagon.

He started down as the rain, matching his pulse, thudded against his shoulders and hat. It came in gusts now like some giant hand heaving occasional handfuls of gravel against him.

He eased the bay forward, up the hogback ridge to his right, circling away from the point where the trail entered the deep valley.

He left the roan in a small, sheltered hollow, tethering it with the lariat to a clump of brush. There too he dried and checked his weapons. Then, mounting again, he eased over the ridge and down into Chato Chavez' hidden valley as the blustering storm darkened the night and the wind howled down the long canyons.

The bay's hooves clattered on unseen stone and the voice called out of the darkness, "Who is there?"

Justice, cursing his luck, slipped from the bay's back and let it walk on. From above he heard the sound of someone moving about and in a minute he saw the dark figure of a man against the sky.

"Who is that?" he called out again uncertainly. The bay had gone on fifty feet or so and then stopped dead, hanging its head. Justice crept nearer to the horse, his pistol in hand, one hand pressed to the rock at his back.

A stone bounced down from above and missed his head by bare inches. Justice didn't move. Holding himself against the rock, he saw the horse lift its head and look uphill. There was a muffled exclamation and then the sentry appeared, rifle in hand, standing on a narrow outcropping above and to the right of Justice.

"Salvador?" He looked at the horse and then swiveled his head until he seemed to be looking directly at Justice, but in the darkness and the rain his eyes did not pick out the motionless man. "Salvador?" he whispered again.

There before him was Salvador's horse, but Salvador had gone riding off that afternoon. Now the horse was back. The guard was a cautious man, but he was also a curious one.

Ruff saw him pull back, retracing his steps, and a long minute later, heard the guard descending some unseen path to the cut. Justice still had not moved. Now he began to ease forward toward the bay. There was apparently only one man up there—the guard had not called to anyone to cover him. One man, and he was just not cautious enough.

Ruff heard a boot scrape over gravel, saw the hat and rifle silhouetted against the frothing sky. The guard was no more than thirty feet away, and now, as he approached the horse, looking down the cut, he closed the gap. Ruff's voice was soft, but it carried well enough for the guard to hear him, to freeze in his tracks.

"Put the gun down, *hombre*, if you wish to live."

The bandit didn't move at first, then slowly his head started to come around, eyes searching the darkness, seeking a target.

"Right now," Justice said. "Put it down or you are a dead man."

Still the guard hesitated, no doubt afraid of what Chavez might do to him. Yet he was not a stupid man and slowly the fingers opened and the rifle clattered to the ground.

Justice stepped from the shadows now, pistol leveled at the bandit's belly.

"Who are you?" the guard demanded. "Do you know whose camp this is?"

Neither question seemed worth answering. "Turn around," Justice told him, "and keep those hands a little higher."

Slowly the outlaw turned and Justice walked to him, lifting his belt gun, tossing it away. "All right," he said, "you can turn back around."

"You are a dead man," the guard hissed. "When Chato Chavez finds you, you are a dead man."

"He won't need to find me," Justice said. "I'm going down there right now to talk to him. I want to know where he sleeps."

"Go to hell," the guard said, and Justice, who had no time for playing games, stepped in and slammed the barrel of his pistol against the bandit's neck. He went down in a heap, a muffled howl of pain escaping his lips. Justice stood over him, the hammer of his Colt drawn back, his grim face weirdly lit by distant lightning.

"You will either answer the question or you will die," Justice said evenly, and the bandit, holding his neck, looked up at the tall man and he believed him.

"There are four cabins," he panted. "Chavez lives in the small one nearest the oak grove."

"Fine," Justice said, smiling without a trace of humor. "Is he alone?"

"He may have a woman with him; besides that, he is alone."

"A woman?"

"Yes. We captured a woman . . . that is what brings you here," the man said with sudden understanding. "You are crazy, then, *señor*, mad as Satan. To challenge Chavez over a woman when there are so many in this world."

"Sure," Ruff said, "crazy." Then he laid the pistol none too gently behind the man's ear and he went out, sprawling in the mud. Justice tied him with his own belt and his shirt. Dragging him a little way, he rolled him into the rocks beside the path.

Then he collected the reins to the bay and led it off the trail as well. The horse stared at him wide-eyed and Justice muttered, "I know, horse, mad as Satan."

Ruff removed the rifle from the saddle boot and set off through the rain, a mad Satan bringing damnation.

9

The rain had stopped but the wind still swirled in the hidden valley where Chato Chavez had his hideout. Ruff Justice, crouched low in the huge old oaks that grew to the west of the stone cabin, heard it shifting the boughs of the trees, cartwheel leaves across the dark earth. But he paid no attention to the wind, the damp, the ominous rumbling of thunder in the distance.

All of his attention was on the cabin; it stood out clearly in the moonlight that spilled through a great rift in the clouds.

Was Elena in there? He had no idea. He could see the little cabin, three others, apparently bunkhouses, some distance away, the wagon, and a shed of some sort.

And that was all. He couldn't see the cattle herd, which had been pushed up into a small canyon; could see no guards, no sign of Cosacha, Miguel, and Carlos. Of Vargas.

He had no plan, only the vague idea that once he managed to get Chato Chavez in his sights, things might work out. Possibly he could hold the bandit king hostage until they were able to get clear. If Chavez played it tough and had to be killed, the game was up for all of them—if it wasn't already over for the four captured men. It could be that the reason Ruff didn't see them was because they were spending a peaceful night out of the rain—under six feet of earth.

He glanced again at the moon, guessing at the time—between three and four A.M.—then, sucking it up, simultaneously cursing himself, Ruff Justice shuttled silently toward the cabin, rifle in hand.

There were sixty feet of open ground to cover, and he half-expected the guns to open up before he made it to the cabin wall, but apparently the rain was keeping the sentries under cover. Panting, shaking with the cold, he found himself suddenly there.

Ruff pressed himself against the stone wall of the cabin, the rifle-held muzzle up across his chest. His eyes searched the shadows, his ears were intently alert for any sound. There was none.

Nothing seemed to move either in the camp or within the cabin itself. Ruff moved forward toward the door. Above him was a narrow window, too high to peer into. From it came a smoky scent—a fire gone dead.

He looked around the corner of the cabin, the wind tugging at his shirt. Nothing. No one seemed to be around. It was as if Chavez had pulled out, but that was impossible. Justice would have seen him— unless there was another way out of the hideout.

He had come too far to alter his plan anyway. There was nothing for it but to proceed. Justice eased toward the door and found the latch string out. The door swung open silently, and Ruff Justice stepped inside Chato Chavez' cabin.

He stood there in the silent darkness, his eyes adjusting, his rifle held out before him, hammer drawn back, finger tense on the cool, curved trigger.

"Close the door," a voice said, "the wind is cold."

Justice saw the man on the bed sit up, scratching his shaggy head. "Hold still, Chavez, I've got a gun on you."

"Yes, I see that," the man answered. "Who are you? What do you want?"

"I want the woman, Chato. I want the cattle and the four men you're holding prisoner."

There was a long silence, then Justice saw the head wag. "No," Chavez said, "you cannot have them."

"Then I'll have you."

"If it must be."

Chavez' voice was startling. Calm, almost gentlemanly. It was cultured and pleasant, yet beneath the surface there was an incredible tension that transmitted itself to Ruff's softer senses. He was in a closed room with a panther.

"Can't we have light," Chavez said. "Light the lamp for me, stranger. You did not tell me your name."

"Light it yourself if you want," Justice said. He wouldn't mind that himself. Chavez was only a shadow now, a patch of gray against the darker gray of the cabin interior. He saw the man stretch out a hand and he warned him.

"Make sure that's a match box you're reaching for."

"Of course," Chavez said.

Ruff saw him fumble with the box, saw him strike the match, which flared up blue and yellow. Chavez lifted the chimney of his bedside lamp and touched the match to the wick, and the room was flooded with yellow light.

The man with the full head of dark, wavy hair, the black eyes, and cleft chin sat there looking back at Ruff with casual interest. He waved out the match and flicked it onto the floor, turning down the wick slightly before replacing the chimney and settling back on his bed, hands behind his head.

"Get up and get dressed," Justice said, "we've got some fast traveling to do."

"It is foul weather outside," Chavez answered with a yawn.

"Tough luck. Get up and get on your feet."

"You came in here alone?" Chavez asked. Ruff didn't answer. "Of course, you must have." He reached under the bed and pulled out his boots.

"Hurry it up."

"I have told you, I am not going anywhere."

"But you are, Chavez. You're going to go with me or you're going to take a bullet right here and now."

"And what would that help?" Chavez asked. "It would not free the woman and the prisoners. It would only get you killed. Besides, I have decided that I like this woman. And the cattle"—he shrugged, rising to pull on his pants—"I must have food for my men. Fifty-two soldiers to feed, my friend. They must eat, and they require much."

"Maybe the government will feed them for you."

"The government? Oh, yes. Most amusing. You are an amusing man, and I suppose a brave one, or you would not be standing here. But, as I have told you, I cannot comply with your demands."

"You'll damn well comply or you'll not live out this night, Chavez."

"We shall see. Ramón?"

Justice felt a cold chill creep up his spine as he realized that Chavez was talking to someone behind him. Unless he was bluffing—but Ramón answered and Justice knew the game was up.

"*Sí,* Chato."

"This man wishes to kill me. If he does, you will kill the woman, do you understand me? First the man and then the woman."

"*Sí,* Chato, I understand."

"Now, what was it you wanted?" Chavez asked, smiling thinly. "You understand what will happen if you do not put that rifle down right now?"

"I understand, you cold-blooded bastard."

"Good. Down then—" Ruff's rifle rattled to the floor. "Now the pistols, I think." The handguns followed and Chavez nodded with satisfaction.

Then he stepped in, his face transforming. Gone was the cool suaveness, the gentlemanly demeanor. He was a dark-eyed demon, his mouth twisted into savage hatred. He backhanded Ruff's face, the blow filling Ruff's mouth with blood. Simultaneously a crushing pain flooded his back. Ramón had jammed the stock of his rifle into Justice's spine, and he went down in a heap.

The room spun before his eyes, light and shadow, weirdly colored by pain. But he could see well enough to see Chavez draw back his booted foot and slam it forward into his ribs, lifting Justice inches from the floor.

Chavez was a wild man now, his eyes protruding from his skull, his jaw clenched so tightly it seemed he would splinter his teeth. The boot landed again and again, this time flush on Ruff's jaw, and he went mercifully under, falling through the velvet tunnel beneath him as Chavez hammered mindlessly on a body that could feel no more pain.

When Ruff next opened his eyes, he knew it was the pain that had shaken him from unconsciousness, demanding that the brain pay heed to the torment of a battered body. He tried to sit up, and the pain, a wall of pain, knocked him down again.

Each breath hurt, bringing a jagged pain to his lungs; each thought hurt. His brain was a caldron of molten metal sloshing around inside a crumbled bag of bone.

He heard voices. Sometimes they seemed miles away, distant and muffled. Then again it would seem that they were screaming in his ears, shouting in some wild, unintelligible language.

He felt as if he had been set afire and then the fire had been beaten out with shovels. There was no escaping the pain, and some merciful mechanism in his mind was triggered, allowing him to fall off again into the limitless tunnel where strange bearded faces mocked him and Chato Chavez' laughter echoed away into eternity.

When he came around again, the pain was still with him, but it seemed just barely possible to endure it—if a man made every movement slowly, carefully.

He began by carefully opening a swollen eye. That was fine—he made it without the world shattering to pieces. With that open eye he lay staring at a packed-earth floor. There was enough light to see that, so his numbed brain decided that it must be daylight outside.

Outside of what? Shifting his line of vision, he saw a plank wall with narrow chinks between the boards. There dull gray light winked at Justice. He could hear the whistling of the wind, and somewhere beyond the wall, voices.

"Can you sit up?"

The voice was familiar, but it was a while before Justice recognized it.

"Carlos?"

"Yes, Ruff, it's me. You damned fool—why didn't you just stay away from here."

"Because," Ruff grunted, trying to sit up, "I am . . . a damned . . . fool."

He was now a damned fool sitting upright, his arms behind him, bracing him up. His head began humming a tuneless little song. His eyes ached.

"Where are we?"

"In a shack at Chavez' hideout. What they call the place is Tepoca Canyon. It's in the middle of the desert, on the edge of hell."

"Where's Elena?"

"I don't know."

"Has Chavez got her?"

"I don't know, Ruff. I told you. I don't know anything except that I was thrown in here four nights ago, and two nights ago you joined us."

"Us?" Ruff's eyes shifted to the corner. There sat Miguel, his long face expressionless. There was a huge welt running across his eye from forehead to cheek. Beside him lay a savagely battered thing, shapeless, blood-encrusted.

"Cosacha?"

"He tried to fight back. They took him out in the

yard and beat him. When they brought him back, he spat in their faces. They took him out again."

"Is he alive?"

"Miguel?" Miguel nodded his head slightly.

Justice touched a hand to his own face, finding it scabbed and swollen. He winced as he ran a finger across a lump above his ear. He had been lucky—they had done their best work on him while he was out.

In the far corner sat another man, hands folded in his lap. His eyes looked back blankly at Ruff Justice.

"So you made it, Vargas?"

He shrugged. "To here."

"The man," Ruff said to Carlos, "Chavez—what does he want?"

"He has said nothing," Carlos answered. Ruff saw that his arm had been splinted and done up in a hasty sling.

"He is mad," Miguel said. "Mad as a man can be."

"Yes," Justice replied, "he is." He recalled the savagery in the bandit's eyes, the sudden change of mood, the glazed expression. "I wonder if we can use that madness."

"Use it?" Vargas said. "Use it for what?"

"To get out of here."

"Out of here?" Miguel's eyebrows drew together. "It is not possible, Mr. Ruff Justice. If you believe that, you are as mad as Chavez."

"Maybe." It had been said before. Maybe he was mad, but . . . "If you think I'm going to sit here and wait to see what sort of tortures, what sort of death Chavez can design for me, then you too are mad, Miguel. No—I won't do that. I can take most anything but sitting and waiting, surrendering."

"You look like you're in shape to start a war," Vargas said ironically.

"I might not get the chance to get into any better shape," Ruff replied, shifting himself so that he leaned against the wall, every joint and muscle, tendon and ligament in his body crying out in silent protest.

It was all well enough to talk, but deep down he knew Vargas was right—they had no chance at all. The only wonder was that Chavez hadn't killed them already, but then, maybe he had something special in mind.

What Ruff had told Vargas was also true, however: he would not sit and wait for death to come. He had seen men do just that, and they always met the death they had expected. It was only the fighter who survived—sometimes.

A check of his boot discovered the skinning knife. They had not found it. His odds had just improved. Instead of being an unarmed, physically battered man alone against fifty-two cutthroat bandits, he was a man with a small knife against the army of Chavez.

That thought was enough to bring a smile to his puffed lips, and he leaned back, closing his eyes as the others stared at him, sure now that they were in the presence of another madman.

At dusk two men came to the cabin. The door was kicked open and the first thing to appear was the muzzle of an angry-looking 10-gauge shotgun.

Then the man entered, easing into the far corner, both hammers of that shotgun wheeled back.

"All right, Esteban," he said, and a second man entered. The camp cook, maybe. At least he was carrying two pails with something that smelled vaguely like food in them. This one was a small, nervous man without much hair. Fifty-one men, Ruff calculated mentally. This one would not fight. He smiled again—he was gaining on the enemy.

The pails were placed down in the center of the earthen floor, and then, covered by the scatter-gun, the cook backed out of the room. The bandit with the shotgun looked them over and then went out, closing the door. A second later they heard a heavy bar being dropped across the door.

"One of them's water," Vargas said, examining the pails. "The other—I don't know what it is except there's a few beans floating on top."

"Eat all of it you can," Justice told them. "We'll need what strength we can muster."

Carlos glanced at Ruff. His face was pale, his arm obviously bothering him tremendously. There was sympathy in Carlos' eyes. Sympathy for the mad.

A ladle had been provided and they took turns using it, gulping down the warm soup—or stew, whatever it was. Ruff took the water bucket to where Cosacha lay. From time to time the Jumano groaned or a limb twitched, but he hadn't opened his eyes or made a single controlled movement of his body.

Ruff peered down at the face, scarcely recognizable as human. He lifted an eyelid and got some response from the pupil. "Cosacha!" Ruff patted his bloody cheek. The only answer was a deep, chesty groan.

"Leave him alone," Vargas said.

"Leave him alone to die?"

"He'll never be any good again," Miguel said. "He's broken up inside. You can tell that."

Ruff ignored them. "Cosacha. Wake up." He cupped a little water in his hand and let it trickle over the Jumano's split, bloodied lips. "Come on. There's work to do."

Cosacha's tongue darted out and his mouth opened, sucking in the moisture. Again he groaned and Ruff cupped another handful of water toward his lips, holding his head up now.

"God's sake, can't you leave the man to die in peace," Vargas shrieked.

"Maybe Cosacha does not want to die in peace— maybe Cosacha does not want to die at all," Ruff answered angrily. "Maybe he's too much man to just give in to death."

"Yes, he is too much man," Vargas answered, "that

is what got him that beating. He wanted to fight back
like you do, Justice, and that is what it got him."

"Leave him alone," Miguel said. "Leave the man to
die, Justice."

"Miguel?" Carlos looked around from the stew
pail, his eyes meeting those of Ruff briefly.

"¿Sí, patrón?"

"Justice is right. Don't say anything else. If we're to
get out of here at all, we've got to believe we can. If
Cosacha must die, then he will, but we haven't the
right to count him as the dead when he's alive."

Miguel nodded silently. Ruff continued to talk to
Cosacha, to try to pull him up out of the depths. He
appreciated Carlos' words, they showed a certain
faith in Ruff. Justice only wished that there was
some way to justify that faith. For just then he was
feeling as low as he could ever remember feeling.
The truth was that Miguel and Vargas were probably right. Cosacha was a dead man already. As were
they all.

10

━━◆━━

"You!"

The door had been flung open and the shotgun-equipped guard had stormed in, followed by two other black-bearded *bandidos* wearing pistols and crossed bandoliers, their eyes tiny, dark, and savage.

The finger was jabbed at Ruff Justice again, and he looked up.

"You come with us. Chato will see you."

"All right," Ruff said lazily. It was a struggle to get to his feet and the bandits watched him with impatience and amusement.

Outside, the night was star-bright, a few ravaged clouds floating past the serrated tip of the high ridge. Across the camp someone was playing a guitar. Ruff let his eyes take in the situation.

There, around a fire, six men passing a bottle, speaking in low voices; beyond the next stone cabin two men walking sentry. Up the narrow feeder canyon Col. Hollingshead's cattle herd. Justice could smell beef roasting as he was marched toward Chavez' cabin, and he knew that the herd had been diminished by one.

The guards halted, one on each shoulder, one going into the cabin. After a minute Ruff heard Chato's voice and the guard reappeared.

"Go in," he said. Justice did so, finding Chavez leaning back in a chair, a bottle of wine on his lap, a pistol beside him on a small table.

"Stand right there," Chavez said.

Elena. She stood in a far corner, hands folded before her, her dark dress dusty, split at one shoulder seam, her hair pinned up, her eyes moist and wide, her lips parting, trembling as she saw Justice.

"Ruff," she managed to say.

"Silence, woman," Chato said, and with a frightened glance at Chavez, she fell silent, turning her eyes downward.

"Has he harmed you, Elena?" Ruff asked quietly.

"Be quiet, Justice, until I have spoken to you!"

"Tell me if he has," Justice went on as if Chato had not interrupted him. "I promise you he'll pay."

"Pay!" Chavez stiffened in his chair, his hand reaching out for the pistol at his side.

"I swear you will pay, Chavez, if you've harmed her. You could shoot me dead, but maybe I'd get to you first. Maybe I'd have the strength to rip your throat out with my bare hands."

"Such a man for talk." Chato laughed. "Is he always like this? He boasts and makes his war talk, yet never have I seen his war."

"You will, Chavez. You'll see it soon enough. If you bury me, I'll come back to haunt you. If you cut my body to pieces, my severed hands will creep across your bed at night and rip your throat from your carcass."

Then Justice saw that he had touched something, some deep and dark fear in Chato Chavez. Just for a moment a shadow of doubt flitted through those brooding eyes, for a moment he seemed a child shaking in the dark; then the old confidence returned.

"You are quite a joker, Mr. Justice."

"Am I?" Ruff's eyes were cold and sober.

"I have something for you." Chato reached beside his chair and tossed Ruff his buckskins. "I am sorry I cannot return your guns."

He looked real sorry. Justice didn't pick up his clothes just then. They lay in a heap at his feet.

"I also have your saddlebags. There was in them a

card with your name on it. It identified you as being of the United States army."

"That's right."

"And what is it you do?"

"I'm a brigadier general. Cavalry."

"The card says you are a scout," Chavez said, smiling thinly.

"Why'd you ask, then?"

"I want to know, Mr. Justice, why you are here, in Mexico."

"Simple. I was escorting those cattle back to Fort Sumner. Those are army property, Chavez. American army property. Unless you want two armies on your tail, I'd advise turning them over and letting us go. If you're nice, I'll see that you get a few head to tide you over."

Chato's face paled. His lips were compressed into a razor-thin line. "I do not like being toyed with, Justice. By any man. I have the beef, I will keep it. The United States, I think, will not send an army into a foreign land to recover either a few steers or a cocky scout."

"In that case you don't know Colonel Hollingshead," Justice said easily. "He'll be coming, all right, as soon as we fail to meet our delivery schedule."

"I admire your imagination," Chavez said. "I wish my mind could so quickly fabricate such tales."

Ruff's little imaginative sally hadn't exactly struck fear into Chato's heart, but just maybe it had planted a small seed of doubt. That was all Ruff wanted, a small doubt here, the shadow of fear there, uncertainty that might spring some hope of release free.

"Then there's the woman," Ruff went on, leaning a shoulder against the wall. "It was a big mistake to take her."

"I do not think so."

"She's on her way to meet her husband, Mr. William Dobbs."

"She has told me she is not married," Chavez said.

"Her soon-to-be husband. Perhaps the lady hasn't told you just who Mr. Dobbs is."

"The head of the Texas Rangers, no doubt," Chavez said, drinking from his bottle.

"No, but he's got connections. He's one of the richest and most powerful men in Texas. He could raise an army ten times the size of yours overnight—and likely will, if he doesn't get his fiancée back."

"You are beginning to tire me, Mr. Justice. I don't believe a word you say. Even if I did believe you, what is the difference? No one knows what has happened to you or to the woman—perhaps the Apaches, perhaps you died from lack of water on the desert. Even if someone did know what has happened, how could they find me here?" He raised his hands in a gesture of confidence.

"They'll know, they'll find you. I wasn't alone, you know."

Elena's eyes flickered to his, and he saw hope building there. Chato looked momentarily uncertain.

"There was a kid named Pablo with us. We were together when you attacked the camp. I set off to follow you. I told Pablo to ride like hell for the border. He had two good horses with him. By now, I figure he's just about made it. And I blazed an easy trail for him to follow back to Tepoca Canyon. No, Chavez, they'll be coming. Soldiers, private warriors, all of them looking for you. The best thing for you to do is turn us loose right now and get your tail out of this area."

Chavez looked at Elena for a long minute, then his eyes shuttled back to Ruff. "I think," he said, "you talk too much, Mr. Justice. You are a wind that blows past me, scattering dust, but not disturbing the rocks. I am a rock, Justice, and I do not believe your foolishness for a minute."

The door behind Justice opened then and a bearded face was thrust in.

"Chato—it is your brother. He is back."

"Alfredo. *Muy bien*, bring him to me. I am through with this liar."

Justice bent and picked up his clothes then, offering a smile for Elena, who still held her head proudly but looked as if at any moment she might collapse.

"Go now, Justice," Chato Chavez said. "Go and sleep, build more dreams to tell me." He laughed then, harshly, at length. Justice turned toward the door just as it opened and the young man with his arm bandaged to the shoulder stepped in.

The man stopped, eyes widening as he saw Ruff Justice. Justice knew him—he had carried the kid forty miles to the town of Zopilote to be cared for. Alfredo, the kid who had come to rob him in the night and then had lain crying, begging for help. Chato's brother.

Ruff clamped his jaw and strode out through the door, hearing the brothers greet each other. Then the door was closed and the three guards walked him back to the shack, where he was shoved in to stand holding his bundle of clothes before the empty eyes of the three prisoners.

"Well?" Carlos asked, and Ruff could only shake his head.

"How is he?" Ruff asked, nodding toward Cosacha as he stripped down and dressed in his buckskins.

"Bad, very bad. He hasn't moved since you left."

Ruff fingered Cosacha's skull, finding nothing broken. His arms and legs also appeared unbroken, but as Miguel had said, he was probably all busted up inside.

"Come on, chief," Ruff said softly, "you can make it. You'll live to fight me again."

There was no response, no movement. Justice again gave Cosacha water while the others sat and brooded. Carlos was shivering. His broken arm had drained him of any strength. That left old Miguel and Vargas, whom Ruff hardly trusted.

A hell of an army. Outside were fifty armed men,

all of them willing if not eager to kill. Escape? Maybe. That left them with a hundred miles of desert to cross on foot. And somewhere out there a beehive of Apaches to get through.

Ruff sat back on his haunches, his mind discovering and then discarding a hundred impossible plans

"Perhaps one of us could get out," Carlos suggested

"Justice?" Vargas asked disparagingly.

"If it could be only one of us, I would want it to be him," the young man said. "Miguel, I am sorry, but you are too old. I am of no use. Vargas—well, who knows if he would come back. You still do not wish to tell us who, what you are? No? Then of course I would choose Justice."

Which was very complimentary, Ruff thought, but didn't solve a damned thing.

"How to get out?" Miguel asked, his long face thoughtful. "Although I agree it must be done soon. Who knows what Chavez may decide to do with us or when?"

"He would have to have a horse," Vargas said.

"I have one hidden," Ruff said. If the roan hadn't broken free of its tether. The odds of that were about even.

"Where could he ride—soon enough?" Vargas asked. He shrugged. "Perhaps if a man could escape he might save his own life, but how could he help the rest of us—or the woman?"

And that was the crux of the matter. Vargas was exactly right. Chavez, in a fury, might simply execute all of them. By the time Justice could return with the federales, the camp would be deserted but for the dead.

It was all highly theoretical anyway. He wasn't outside riding for help. He was locked in this shack, which was well-guarded.

"We will kill them all, Justice," the voice beside Ruff said. It was a low, wavering voice, and it was a time before they realized that Cosacha had spoken.

Ruff turned and looked down at the Indian, seeing the gleam in those puffed eyes, and he smiled.

"Back from the dead," Ruff said, crouching down.

"Not quite, Ruff Justice. Not yet. I think I have one foot in hell and the devil he is tugging at it. God, I am thirsty, give me water, *por favor.*"

Justice brought the bucket over, and propping Cosacha's head up on one of his knees, he gave him drinks from his cupped hand.

"I swear I will kill them all, Ruff Justice."

"Yes. You and I together."

"What they have done to me! The bastards," Cosacha growled, then he fell to choking, gasping horribly. "My guts. Very bad. I'm on fire. More water, please."

Justice gave it to him.

It was then that they heard the distant shots being fired. A dozen of them in rapid succession. Their heads came up sharply. They sat in the darkness of the hut, listening intently. Hope rose up and then fell away.

"Apaches," Carlos guessed.

"Federales."

"Not enough shots for the federales."

The gunfire had died away. There was nothing but the hurried, whispered sounds of the guards outside the hut.

"Maybe nothing," Cosacha said. "Maybe killing cattle for slaughter."

"Maybe."

"In the middle of the night!" Vargas scoffed. His eyes were lighted with excitement. "No, my friends, someone is pricking at Chato Chavez. There were only a few shots—perhaps we shall hear more. Perhaps tonight we shall be free."

But there were no more shots fired that night.

Silence fell over the camp. Inside the shack they heard nothing. Justice had made up his mind to take matters into his own hands, and the first matter was getting the hell out of that shack.

"What are you doing?" Vargas asked. Justice had scooted up nearer to the wall, his feet against the planks. He held up a hand, silencing Vargas. By listening closely Ruff could hear the guard outside shuffle past on his rounds. He now waited as the footsteps came nearer and then died away.

"Cough," Justice told Carlos, who did so tentatively. As he did, Ruff smashed his feet against the planks, prying them free of their nails, but only slightly.

"Again, louder," Justice said, and this time Carlos broke into a genuine fit of coughing, deep and loud. Ruff kicked out with both feet again, seeing some success. The bottoms of the planks had pulled away an inch or two from the runner.

Ruff held up a hand for Carlos to be quiet. He could hear the guard now, walking more slowly, more stealthily. Vargas was looking at Ruff as if he were mad. Miguel's expression was sour and tight.

The guard went on and Ruff nodded to Carlos, who began again. Ruff lifted his feet and kicked again and the door opened behind him.

"What the hell's going on in here?" the guard growled. He had his shotgun leveled at Justice, who had put on his most innocent expression. "Well?"

A second Chavez man intervened. He stepped into the room, pointed a finger at Justice, and said, "This one. Chato will see him again—and this time the conversation will not be so very polite. Up on your feet, tall man. You go to meet the devil."

11

Ruff rose, seeing Carlos' grim face, hearing a low growl from Cosacha. He walked to the door, prodded by a shotgun muzzle. Outside, it was cold and dark. The clouds had come in again and it looked like more rain. The wind teased the fringes of Ruff's buckskins, tugged at his hair.

"I'll take him," the man beside Justice said.

"Alone?"

"What did I tell you!"

"All right. What do I care?" The man with the shotgun shrugged and went back to his post.

"Let's go," the other said.

Ruff walked along toward the oaks, looking neither right nor left. When they made the dark, shadowed trees, his guard said, "Take off! Now."

"I can't do it, Alfredo."

"Are you crazy?" Chato's brother hissed angrily. "You gave me my life at Zopilote. Now I'm giving you yours. Take off, Justice. Run for it and you might make it on a night like this."

"I can't do it. Not without the woman and those men back there."

"*Ai, hombre, estás loco*! A man gives you your life and you throw it away."

"I can't go without those people, Alfredo. Can't you understand that?"

"I can understand it, but I can do nothing about it, Justice. The woman is with my brother. How can I get her free? No—Chato would kill me for this, if he knew, but he won't know. There is no reason for him to suspect that I let you go. He doesn't know about Zopilote. Take my gun. Hit me and go. I will say you escaped."

"No."

"I can do nothing else, Justice," Alfredo said. The wind lifted the dark hair from his scalp. There seemed to be genuine anguish in his voice.

"What was that shooting we heard?" Ruff wanted to know.

"Federales. Only a few. The lookouts below panicked and started shooting. Some of the soldiers escaped to carry word back to their commander. Chato has decided to desert this camp. We leave at dawn for Comanche Peak."

"Comanche Peak?"

"*Sí*, it is in the heart of the badlands. A terrible, savage place where nature rules, where men do not go of their own choice. There is water in only one place. There Chato can hold out forever if need be. You see, Justice, it must be tonight that you make your escape or not at all."

"Then it won't be, Alfredo. I can't leave them."

"They mean so much to you?"

"Some of them I hardly know," Ruff answered, "but we're in this together. I don't pull off leaving people in trouble. You ought to know that."

"Yes, I do know that. I have made the offer, Justice," the kid said. "I owe you no more."

"Never said you did."

"I have fulfilled my obligation."

"All right. Take me back, then."

Alfredo started to speak, tried to, but he shut his mouth and stood shaking his head in disbelief. He looked at the revolver in his hand and then at Ruff. "You are mad, *hombre*," he said finally. "Come, I will take you back."

"Alfredo—what's he keeping us alive for? What does Chato intend to do with us?"

"I do not know." The kid shrugged. "You must understand Chato. He is . . . not right sometimes. His moods come and go. He can be pleasant, most pleasant, then again he is a savage. I believe he doesn't honestly know what to do with you. Others he has shot out of hand. You, he keeps prisoner. For how long, no one can tell."

There was no more conversation. Ruff was taken back to the shack and locked inside once again. He sagged to the floor near the loosened planks. He lifted his feet and then heard the guard's voice through the wall.

"At the next cough I will empty this shotgun through those planks."

"No matter, Ruff Justice," Vargas said. "What would we have done if we had gotten outside? The five of us without a weapon between us?"

"Did you find out anything?" Carlos asked. He looked weaker now. His face was contorted with the pain of that broken arm.

"Chavez is moving out in the morning," Briefly Ruff told them what he had learned.

"And us? Are we moving with him?" Vargas asked.

"Only Chavez knows that," Justice had to tell him. Then he scooted up against the wall and tried to sleep, knowing as the rest of them did that this might very well be their last night on earth.

They came with guns and ropes in the cold, pre-dawn gray. Entering the shack, they ordered everyone to their feet. Cosacha had to be helped up, but he made it, standing there, glowering, dark eyes peering out of a face that had purple-and-yellow bruises covering most of it.

"Hands out," the guard said, and they obliged. There wasn't much point in arguing with those shotguns.

Ruff waited his turn, seeing Carlos nearly faint with agony as they jerked his broken arm around so that his wrists could be tied. Justice was next. They tied him with rawhide, drawing the knots tight. The hands were tied in front, leading Ruff to believe they were going to be doing some riding.

"Now, out," the guard said, and they shuffled out into a bleak gray world. The wind pushed heavy, leaden clouds past the high ridges. The dawn, if it could be called that, was only a gradual lessening of the blackness in the eastern skies.

The wagon was hitched, Ruff saw. And that was Elena sitting in the box, hands clasped. Beside her was Alfredo Chavez. Across the valley floor Ruff saw the cattle being moved out, herded by twenty bandits who whistled and swung lariats overhead.

"My God," Carlos said, "he's running with the cattle. Is he crazy?"

"Very likely," Justice said. Justice was pushed none too gently forward, and they came upon the string of horses guarded by three more Chavez men. The gray was there and it looked around disdainfully at Ruff, its white face chastising.

"Each man to a horse," their guard said, and each man mounted. Cosacha needed some help, as did Carlos. Ruff managed to swing up easily and he sat his gray, watching the wagon turn to follow the herd up the canyon. So there was another way, a second trail that was very likely known only to Chavez. The federales, when they came, would approach with utmost caution, working their way through the rocks, expecting fierce resistance. Then they would arrive at the camp and find it empty. Chavez would be on the loose once more, and at that point no one could really blame the Mexican commander for turning around and going home.

Justice's horse was tethered to a lead animal by a twenty-foot-long lariat. Now the bandit in charge of him swung up, kneed his horse, and led out in the wake of the cattle. The wind blustered down the canyon, spraying them with dust from the herd.

They rode up toward the crest of the ridge through

a winding gorge, frequently waiting while the cattle were squeezed two by two through an impossibly narrow, high-rising cut. The clouds had settled to the bottom of the canyon, and disembodied heads floated past, people and horses appearing and disappearing like phantoms.

By noon they had eased out of the gorge and onto the floor of a valley surrounded by lines of convoluted, barren hills. Nothing seemed to grow there, not even the ubiquitous cholla cactus.

Here water had rushed at intervals off the flanks of the hills, scoring deep washes across the land. No vegetation slowed the flash floods sweeping off the highlands, and though the waters flowed only perhaps twice or three times a year, when they ran, they came with the force of locomotives, carrying huge boulders along, cutting away at the raw, unprotected earth, destroying anything unlucky enough to be in the way of the wall of water.

Ahead stood Comanche Peak, its jagged head thrust into the gray masses of rolling clouds. A raw, time-scoured, savage landform like something out of the earth's primeval past, it stood deep red, atavistic, against the storm-tossed skies.

It had begun to rain again, not heavily, but with sporadic flurries. Needles of silver rain jabbed at their faces and then were quickly gone. The earth steamed, a low hazy fog had settled in the washes.

The first Apache rose up out of the gulley to Ruff's right and shot his escort through the head. Ruff ducked to the side of his horse reflexively, seeing the second and third Apaches emerge from the gulley to open fire on Chato's men.

Chavez himself bellowed with rage and turned with a pistol in each hand, firing away at the Apaches, who were now charging the bandits.

Horses went to hind legs, danced away, shied from the sudden apparitions. The Apaches, wildly painted, screaming ululating war cries, fired as they ran. One man, using a repeating rifle, managed to score a triple hit on the dead run. Two bandits fell from their horses, one of them being dragged by his horse across the ground, and a third Chavez man had a horse shot from under him.

The bandits had their rifles out now and the firing was intense, the staccato sound deafening. Black smoke mingled with the ground fog and drifted past Justice.

Ruff was off his horse now, falling once, cursing his bound hands. He was beside his escort now, and rolling the bulky body of the bandit aside, Ruff came up with his six-gun, firing full into the chest of a charging Apache, who was blown back as if jerked by invisible wires.

Ruff crouched then, taking a moment to slip the skinning knife from his boot and sever the rawhide thongs as the bullets flew past him and the gray shied away in terror.

Justice fired from one knee three times in the direction of a knot of Apaches who were firing indiscriminately at cattle, horses, men. Ruff hit one in the hip and saw him try to drag himself away, smearing the earth beneath him with maroon blood.

Justice caught a horse that danced past, stepping on its reins in its confusion and panic. He got behind the shoulder of the animal and fired again, lifting himself by the horse's neck as it raced toward the front of the column.

Elena was there, still all right. They had thrown her into the back of the wagon, and Justice, letting go of the horse's neck at the run, leaped up and into it.

To come face to face with an Apache who had come over the box and into the wagon bed. Justice fired into his face and the Apache was blown back, to land on the back of the wagon team. The horses lurched forward, but the wagon did not move. The brake was on hard and the horses could only prance and whinny in confusion.

The Apache had dropped his rifle—a .44 Henry—and Ruff tossed the empty pistol aside as he took it up.

"Just keep down," he told Elena. She looked at him, wide-eyed, her lip trembling. She just couldn't maintain that proud bearing here, now, and Ruff didn't blame her. He lay beside her, his head and the rifle up over the tailgate. Outside, the battle continued furiously. Ruff saw an Apache take a bandit from his horse and begin scalping him before the bullet from somewhere ripped into the Apache's belly.

Ruff saw that Carlos was down—dead or injured, he couldn't tell. Cosacha simply sat his horse, looking around him as if it were all a play put on for his benefit.

Chavez was at the heart of the battle: now Ruff saw him fire across his body as his big black horse held its position. Chavez seemed to see on all sides of him at once, and he was as good a hand with a pistol as Ruff Justice had seen—and Ruff had seen some.

What Chato couldn't see was the Apache running low to the ground, coming up behind him; and no one is good enough to shoot what he doesn't see. Chavez was going to be a dead man in another few seconds. He had perhaps four more heartbeats left to work his will on the earth and its inhabitants. Perhaps one thump of that black heart left when Ruff Justice settled the bead of his front sight on the Indian's chest and fired.

The Indian had actually reached Chavez. His hand gripped the bandit leader's leg and Ruff saw Chavez spin around, lift his pistol, and then hold off as the Apache slowly slid to the ground, dead.

Then Chato's head came around and he looked at the wagon, the only place the shot could have come from. He gave no indication that he saw Justice, his

expression did not change. Chavez simply got back
to work, fighting back the Apache attack.

When it was over, there were thirteen dead men
on the ground. All of them were Chato's soldiers.
Vargas, Carlos, and Cosacha had made it unscathed,
despite the fact that they were weaponless. Carlos
had fallen from his rearing horse and elected to stay
there, for the pain from his jolted arm immobilized
him.

Ruff stood beside the tailgate, holding Elena's hand.
"Why did you do it, Ruff?" she asked, her eyes deep,
questioning, her hand fluttering beneath his. "Why
help that demon survive to kill again?"

"I don't know. Maybe I prefer the demon I know
to the one I don't know. It wouldn't have changed
anything to let Chavez die. Someone else would have
taken over, maybe someone who couldn't keep these
men in line."

"In line?" Elena shook her head.

"Do you know how they look at you, woman?"
Ruff asked sharply. "There'd be a hell of a lot more
than looking if it wasn't for the fact that Chavez
keeps them away."

"Oh," Elena said weakly, then she shuddered, perhaps imagining it vividly. "That's the reason . . . ?"

"Maybe." It was a damned good reason, but Justice wasn't sure if it was the real one. It may have
been nothing more than battlefield instinct. They
had chosen up sides, and for the moment he and
Chato were on the same side. You don't let them get
one of your people, even if you don't happen to care
for him.

Chavez himself rode up, flanked by two riders.
His big black horse blew and stamped. "Get back
where you belong, Justice," was all he said.

Justice stood looking at him, his hip cocked to one
side, the wind drifting his long hair across his face,
the Henry rifle in hand. Suddenly he grinned, tossed

the rifle to Chavez, and walked away, the black eyes of Chato Chavez boring holes in his back.

It took the rest of the afternoon to round up the cattle once more, and Carlos Trujillo, sitting a sorrel horse, grumbled, "They've lost at least twenty head, dammit."

"What do you care, Señor Trujillo?" Cosacha asked. "You can't be crazy enough to think that you still have any chance in the world of recovering your beef. Not now!"

"Can't I?" Trujillo answered. His chin lifted proudly, his eyes turning toward the Jumano Indian. "Why can't I, Cosacha? A man has to have hope. Very well, my hope is that I shall yet get my cattle to the United States and sell them for enough money to allow me to keep my rancho."

"But it is a dream that is impossible," Cosacha argued. "Me, I wish only to stay alive—at least there is a small chance of that."

"If I must dream, I shall dream big. Besides, it is not madness, not an impossibility, although I do not see now how it could be done. But ask your friend, Ruff Justice, ask him, Cosacha, if it is madness."

"Well?" Cosacha was grinning, the expression bizarre on his puffed, bruised face. "What do you say, Ruff Justice?"

"We'll get 'em there," Justice said, and his voice was utterly sober, his blue eyes hard with determination. "I was sent to do a job, Cosacha, I'll do it."

"All crazy," Cosacha said, waving a hand in a gesture of futility. "I am in the company of madmen, a prisoner of madmen, and I think going slowly mad myself."

They moved on once again, riding through the dense ground fog toward Comanche Peak. Every man rode with a touch of fear in his heart. The Apaches had struck once, they would strike again, and with the covering fog it could be at any time, from any direction. You would not even see death coming, just the shadow of an arrow, the echoing report of a rifle as you toppled from your horse.

Ruff's hands had been tied again, and again his horse was tethered to another. He rode silently on, the fog heavy on his shoulders, able to see little beyond his horse's head. Cosacha was beside him, sullen, battered, vengeful.

They worked their way into the hills, which clustered at the base of the peak now, once making a false start up a box canyon in the fog. The entire herd, the riders, prisoners, and wagon had to be turned around in a narrow area between two high-rising bluffs. It was there that Ruff spoke to Cosacha.

"Do we go?"

Cosacha looked at Ruff. "What do you mean?" The Indian's eyes searched the fog-draped bandits, all now busy with turning the herd.

"Chavez will kill us eventually. This is not like the shack. We have horses. In the fog there is a chance."

"And a chance of getting killed, *hombre*."

"Certainly."

Cosacha smiled. "Then we ride for Saltillo?"

"Then we take the cattle. Free the others and continue our journey."

"It can't be done," Cosacha hissed.

"Maybe not." Ruff sat his horse, his tied hands resting on the pommel, looking at the bandits, who, cursing, raging, turned the herd and then barely got out of its way. "But I must try, Cosacha. Are you with me?"

"The others?" Cosacha asked, nodding toward Vargas, Carlos, and Miguel, who sat patiently waiting.

"No. Carlos' arm is of no use. Miguel, I'm afraid is just a little over the hill. Vargas—well, who knows about Vargas. Myself I trust, and you."

"You are going to do this, then, no matter what I say."

"That's right."

Cosacha sighed, then his face split into a toothy

grin. "All right, I am with you—why, I do not know. It is a fool's plan. Tell me what it is we are to do, and let us do it before sanity returns."

"Give me your hands," Justice told him. "I may not be able to reach you later." Cosacha, glancing around at the occupied guards, leaned toward Ruff's horse as Justice, twisting down, got a hold of his knife and slit one strand of the Indian's bonds.

"And now?" Cosacha asked, still smiling.

"Now we wait for a chance," Justice told him, "and when it comes, we take it—it's liable to be the last we get."

"*Si, amigo*, that is so. Do you know, Ruff Justice," Cosacha said, straight-faced, "with each passing day I regret more the fact that I let you beat me the day we fought."

Ruff was beginning to regret it himself—without that small victory Carlos would have had no vaqueros, they would never have started this drive, they would not have met Chato Chavez. And if Ruff's father hadn't met his mother . . .

You could carry such thinking too far. There was no time for it anyway. The guards led off through the thickening fog that swarmed over the flanks of Comanche Peak, and Justice, his eyes flickering one last time to those of the big-shouldered Jumano, felt the gray move forward, felt his heart begin to swell in his rib cage, felt the cold chill that had its source somewhere deeper than the fog pressing around them. It was the chill of death, and it was about to descend.

12

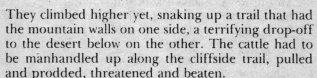

They climbed higher yet, snaking up a trail that had the mountain walls on one side, a terrifying drop-off to the desert below on the other. The cattle had to be manhandled up along the cliffside trail, pulled and prodded, threatened and beaten.

The bandits were in foul spirits. It didn't help things any when the wagon proved to be too wide for the trail and the two outside wheels dropped with a sickening crack over the lip of the ledge and sat there on a broken axle.

Elena, shivering, was helped down, what supplies they could carry loaded onto their horses, and the wreck of the wagon shoved over to careen down the slope, bounce, roll, and be smashed to kindling against a knobby outcropping some two hundred feet below.

Elena was helped aboard one of the dead men's horses, and they pressed on. The day grew dark and still the clouds refused to lift. The wind was a howling beast raging up the slopes, clawing at them.

They acheived a sort of plateau, a nearly flat shoulder of the mountain, about fifty acres of grassless red rock notched into the peak.

There it seemed that Chavez would rest, and Justice thought he had let the opportunity go by, but the bandit leader pressed on again.

It was growing very dark. Now and then a red, shimmering sliver of the dying sun showed through the clouds, but it was always quickly extinguished.

Again they climbed the face of the peak, the ancient trail winding higher into the time-eroded mountain. They had dipped down into a little hollow and were again starting up along a sheer stretch of trail. The road bent back upon itself, around a stack of red boulders. The fog wafted up the canyon, the horses were moving at a cautious walk. Cosacha was just beside Ruff.

Ruff Justice sucked in a deep breath and reached for his knife. Holding it with his fingertips, he awkwardly sawed his bonds away. Then, gripping the lead line, which went from his horse's neck to his escort's saddle, he cut that. Ruff handed the knife to Cosacha, who did the same. Then, in the fog and darkness both men simply slipped from the trail, walking their horses into the rocks.

They had gone fifty yards when a shout was raised. There were a few minutes while the bandits called back and forth that Ruff thought they would come after them. He sat his horse beside Cosacha in that jumble of boulders, peering at the wall of dark clouds, only a knife as a weapon.

"They're going on," Cosacha whispered after a minute.

Ruff nodded, though it was doubtful Cosacha, as near as he was, could see it. Chavez had to go on. He had that herd halted on a narrow trail, darkness falling rapidly, weather conditions abominable.

Besides, as much as he must have hated to let them escape, he knew that there was just nothing much two men could do against his army.

"Now?" Cosacha whispered.

"Wait a minute," Ruff said. And they waited, clothed in darkness, the visibility so poor that Justice could not see his horse's head. They waited and they listened, and after a while they could hear nothing at all. Nothing but the wind chanting in the canyons.

"All right, let's go on, but stay alert. Chato may have left some friends behind."

"Why would he, *hombre*? No one could be crazy enough to follow him up that mountain."

"That might be the way his thinking goes," Ruff agreed, "but don't forget he knows how badly I want the woman out of there." Ruff walked his horse forward slowly. It was no good, he had to swing down and walk, leading the horse.

Cosacha had resigned himself to things, apparently; he said nothing as Ruff walked up that long wind-blown trail in the utter darkness, following Chavez. He simply plodded along behind, leading his own horse.

They were above three thousand feet when the land began to change noticeably. The trail widened and then dipped down, and Ruff began to notice grass and here and there the dark, fog-glossed form of a cedar tree. The moon had poked a rift through the cloud cover and it beamed down. The jagged tip of Comanche Peak, above them another two thousand feet, showed distinctly. The valley floor was lost in shadow and cloud across most of its length.

"Ruff." Cosacha's voice was a low warning, and Justice reined up, following the Jumano's pointing finger with his eyes. Two shadowy figures moved toward them out of the iron-black night and Justice slipped from his gray's back, racing for the jumbled boulders beside the trail. Cosacha turned his horse, and taking the reins to Justice's gray, he rode for the scattered timber to the north.

They couldn't have seen the Jumano, but the bandits must have heard him because they slapped spurs to their mounts and took off down the trail toward Justice. There was no fear whatsoever in the hearts of Chato's men. Why should there be? The two prisoners were unarmed.

But they weren't. This world is a mass of weaponry, taken all in all. Before guns men used clubs and stones to kill one another. It's doubtful the murder rate would drop without guns. A knife will do, a broken bottle, a horse, a little poison—the ways are infinite, subject only to the limitations of the malefactor's imagination.

Ruff had some imagination. He crawled out onto the boulders, seeing the smoky shadows of the riders charging downslope toward his position. Ruff shifted and hefted a head-sized rock from the many on the stack. Then he waited, the rock upraised, and with their attention on the direction Cosacha had taken, with the fog cover, they didn't even see Justice as he timed his throw and let go of the boulder, heaving it toward the onrushing horsemen. It caught the first man flush on the temple, smashing his skull. He fell, his horse dancing away in panic. The second bandit started spraying the boulders around Ruff with lead, the ricochets whining off angrily into the stormy night.

Justice had gone flat and he stayed there, listening, watching. He heard nothing but the stamping of an impatient horse's feet, then the creak of saddle leather as the bandit dismounted.

Ruff backed away from the edge and started working backward down the boulders. He had gone only about halfway when he heard the pebbles trickle downslope, heard the solid click of a hammer being drawn back.

"Come on down. I see you."

That was doubtful in the darkness, but Justice was in no position to make a break for it, trusting to that assumption. He was pinned to the side of the stack of boulders, and he lay perfectly still, eyes probing the thick fog.

"Come on out, I said" the bandit repeated. It was the last sound he was to make. Outside of a horrible gurgling sound that caused Justice to wince, his stomach to tighten.

"I have him," Cosacha said, and Ruff went on down.

The bandit was lying at the big man's feet, his

head twisted around on what was obviously a broken neck. Cosacha bent and picked up the Winchester the bandit had dropped. He hesitated a moment, the rifle in his hand, and Justice simply watched, remembering the night someone had emptied a gun into his bed. He thought now that he knew who it had been. All the evidence pointed that way.

"Come on." Cosacha tossed him the rifle. "We go now."

The Jumano unstrapped the man's gun belt and gave that to Ruff as well. Leading the horse, they returned to the trail, where Cosacha crouched down over the bandit Justice had killed.

"Ugh," Cosacha said, looking at the flattened skull. "I thought I killed my man ugly. You are mean, Justice. Plain mean."

"My momma liked me."

"Yes, you were very young then. She did not know what you would become." Clicking his tongue, Cosacha lifted the bandit's guns.

They recovered the other horses, making four in their string. "It's coming," Justice said as they mounted once more.

"You are satisfied with the odds now?" the Jumano asked dryly.

"They're coming down. The Apaches eliminated thirteen men. Now two more are gone."

"Fifteen from fifty-two."

"Seventeen—I never did tell you about the earlier ones."

"Ai! Bloodthirsty." Cosacha laughed.

"But one came back—Alfredo Chavez."

"Thirty-six men against us, then."

"Thirty-five."

"My arithmetic is not good, but it is thirty-six."

"I never counted the cook, Cosacha. No, it's thirty-five."

"Well, if you don't count the cook . . ." Cosacha spread his hands and laughed. "You are a wild man,

Justice, but I do not remember the last time I enjoyed myself so much."

"Probably the last time you scalped somebody."

"That is not funny, Justice. The Jumanos haven't taken scalps for a hundred years. Of course, on special occasions—" Then he laughed again, a deep booming laugh, but Justice had turned suddenly sober.

"Come on, let's do what there is to be done, Cosacha. The man's got the army beef, he's got my friends, and he's got my woman. Now he can have me—horns, hide, and all—fully loaded."

The rain began to fall as they rode higher toward the Comanche Peak camp of Chato Chavez. By the time they had ridden a mile, it was coming down in torrents, like hordes of malevolent angels dumping bucketfuls of water on their shoulders.

There was no trail to be seen, there was no mountain, nothing but a heavy iron screen of icy rain thundering down. Justice, remembering how they had prayed these clouds would move in and deliver them from the sweltering heat of the desert, managed a faint ironic smile. There must have been lookouts posted, men watching for Justice and Cosacha, but they never saw them.

They couldn't even see the camp as they crested a low, ragged hill, but Cosacha reached out and gripped Ruff's arm.

"Just ahead," he said. "Smell them?"

And Justice *could* smell them, though it hadn't penetrated to his conscious mind until the Jumano pointed it out. Hundreds of wet, steaming animals. The herd.

Ruff pulled off to the right, circling along the flank of the near hill, Cosacha following him as the lightning scored the skies, illuminating briefly the jagged peak towering over them.

Ruff found a sort of alcove, a shallow cave with an overhang carved into the hillside, and he guided his gray into it, waiting for the Indian to catch up.

"You have an idea? I hope." Cosacha wiped the rainwater from his face. A thin sheet of water ran over the lip of the cave roof and fell in a veil to the cold, dark earth.

Ruff swung down from his horse and stood peering out at the darkness. "I can see a log cabin."

"Yes. One building. There, under those pines, you will see tents pitched."

The Jumano had the eyes of a cat. It was a long while before Justice could even make out the pines, let alone the vaguely lighter blotches that were the the tents Chato's men had pitched.

"These men are crazy, Justice. What a way to live, eh? The law chases you from one camp to the next. You sleep out in weather like this. All for the chance of being killed on payday."

Justice was listening, but his mind was elsewhere. Now, as the rain lifted slightly, he could make out the trail, like a glossy blue snake winding between two rocky crowns toward the pines beyond. It was the twin peaks that had his attention.

"Come on," Justice said, swinging a leg over. Cosacha, who had given up asking questions, followed Ruff out into the rainy, windswept night.

They reached the pinnacles in half an hour. They approached cautiously, for it was there, if anywhere, that Chavez should have posted guards.

"What do you think?" Ruff asked finally.

"Think?" Cosacha spread his hands. "I think nothing. What is on your mind now?"

"It wouldn't be difficult to close this pass, is what I'm thinking."

"Maybe not." Cosacha looked at the peaks. They faced each other across the narrowest of trails. Like all the rest of the hills in this country, they were nothing more than stacks of weathered boulders held together by a minimum of soil—and that soil was nothing but thin mud now.

"What do you want to do, Ruff Justice? Close the pass so that none of Chato's men can escape us?"

"Something like that," Ruff said quietly. He just sat his horse, looking at the rain-glossed boulders. Then, satisfied, he nodded his head in decision. "You're going to have a long wet night, Cosacha."

"That is all I was looking forward to anyway, Ruff Justice."

"I want you to poke around here—keep an eye open, there's bound to be guards somewhere."

"What am I poking around for?"

"The best place to start a landslide. Loose boulders, soft slopes, key rocks loose on their moorings."

"A landslide." Cosacha sighed, staring bleakly at Ruff Justice. "And when do I start this landslide?"

"Right after the herd comes through," Justice said. Then to Cosacha's astonishment he winked, grinned, turned the gray, and headed off down the long slopes toward the outlaw camp.

"He is right about one thing," the Jumano said to himself, "this will be a very long night. Very long, if I am waiting for him to bring the cattle through." Shaking his head, wishing that he was back in that warm house with Rosalia, Cosacha got heavily down from the saddle and, rifle in hand, began moving through the rocks.

Justice guided his gray into the pine forest. The trees were deep, dark, and somber. The outlaw camp was still and silent. There were no fires, no signs of movement. The wind creaked through the pines. Great drops of water fell from the boughs and plopped down the back of Ruff's neck.

He emerged slowly from the deep shadows and sat at the verge of the forest, staring down through the rain. The cabin would be Chato's. Likely that was where Elena was. And Alfredo?

Across the clearing, at the edge of the trees, a dozen tents were pitched. Cold, unhappy men sleeping or trying to sleep in them. Bunched in the clearing were the cattle, heads bowed, almost motionless.

Where the prisoners were Justice could not guess from that position. He eased forward through the cloud shadows, eyes seeking. Two riders. It was a time before he picked them out, but he finally saw them. These were the night riders watching the herd. Their hats were tugged low, their collars up, rifles across their saddlebows. They were tired and cold, wishing they were somewhere else, and for the first time Ruff actually began to believe this scheme might work.

Leaving the gray, he rushed forward on foot, going to his belly as one rider, circling the herd, came near. Near, but not near enough. Ruff crawled through the rain-heavy grass, his hands wooden with the cold.

He worked into a shallow wash and lay there, eyes peering through his hanging hair, the grass, at the near rider. Slowly he slipped his knife from his boot, leaving the rifle on the grass beside him.

The horse loomed up large and dark, its flanks lacquered with rain, its head bowed as it trudged in an endless circle around the dark bulk of the herd.

Justice drew his legs up under him and moved. Six quick steps. He thought that the guard's head was starting to come around, that he was starting to react, but in a moment he could not react to anything.

Justice vaulted over the horse's rump and landed on its back as the bandit started to spin around. Already Ruff's hand was over his mouth, however; already the knife had dug deeply, finding warmth on that night. The warmth of blood. The bandit toppled over and Ruff grabbed the horse's reins, halting it.

He slipped to the ground and quickly put on the man's coat and hat, eyes flickering to the far side of the herd where the second rider worked his rounds.

In seconds Ruff was in the saddle, his hat tugged low, his slicker collar up, effectively hiding his face.

He rode casually toward the far side of the herd, his eyes alert and searching without seeming to be so. What time would they change the guard? When would the men in some of those tents be rousted?

There wasn't a lot of point in worrying about that. Justice walked his horse toward the second guard. The skinning knife was in Justice's hand, cool and efficiently deadly.

"*¿Qué pasó?*" The guard asked, turning toward Ruff.

"*Nada. Muy Frío, ¿no?*"

The guard seemed to stiffen at the sound of Ruff's words. His accent? The tone of his voice? Something had tipped the other off. Ruff was within six feet of the man now, however, and it was too late.

He leaned over as if to peer into Ruff's face as they drew even, and again the knife did its deadly work. It flicked out like a snake's tongue, and the outlaw, his face blank with astonishment, his throat slit, slid from his saddle to land softly on the ground, dead.

Ruff felt no pity for the man, nor for any of the others. They had set themselves quite deliberately on the side that opposes law and its restraints. They had stepped outside of the rules. They were rapists, murderers, thieves, each of them waiting his violent end. To some of them it had come a little sooner than they had expected.

Justice turned, leading the second horse. In minutes he was beside the log cabin where presumably Chato Chavez slept.

It was then that Justice nearly blundered. Dropping from the horse, he stepped around the corner of the cabin, to be out of the line of sight from the doorway. He darted around the corner and directly into the path of a bandit.

The man was big, carried a shotgun in his fists,

and had about ten seconds more of his life to live. As he saw Justice, the scatter-gun started to come up. It was a mistake—if he had fired from his waist, he would have blown Justice in two and ended the bloody raid.

As it was, Justice had time to react. The muzzle of the rifle in his hands came up hard, catching the outlaw under the jawbone. With all of Ruff's strength behind it, it tore through flesh and muscles, penetrating into the outlaw's mouth, tearing a savage wound.

The bandit dropped the scatter-gun and fell back, gagging, clutching at the muzzle of the rifle, which was buried in his throat. Justice stepped to him and finished the job with his knife.

Standing, panting, Ruff looked around and immediately saw the reason the guard had been posted there. A tent, invisible from the far side of the cabin, had been pitched there, and as Ruff approached it, Carlos Trujillo's gaunt face appeared. He was tied hand and foot, as were Vargas and Miguel. The old man appeared to have taken a beating. Ruff, motioning for silence, cut them free, and they sat there, rubbing the circulation back into wrists and ankles as Ruff crouched, peering out the tent flap into the stormy night.

"Where's Elena?" he asked in a whisper, and Carlos pointed toward the cabin.

"In there. With Chavez and his brother."

"Are you crazy!" Vargas asked too loudly. "They'll kill us all now, we haven't a chance."

"Shut up," Justice said savagely. There was still blood on his hands and Vargas saw it. He nodded slowly, taking deep breaths to calm himself.

"What do we do?" Carlos asked. He was green around the gills—that arm wasn't getting any better. Likely it would have to come off in the end, assuming they ever made it far enough to find a doctor.

"There's two horses outside. Miguel—you've got the most Injun in you—you'll find my horse about

five hundred feet north, down a little draw. Get it."
He tossed the old man the scatter-gun, handed Vargas
the rifle.

"Do you have a horse?" Carlos asked.

"Don't worry about me. I'll come by one. Listen
now and I'll tell you what I want done."

When he had finished, Vargas just sat there staring.
"It can't be done. You can't mean it. You'll have us
fighting thirty or forty men, skilled men."

"They won't fight while they're sleeping, Vargas.
We're fighting only those who are up and alert, and
that's damned few—for now. Everything has to be
done silently. If it's not, then we've had it."

"We could just slip out now."

"I'm not leaving the herd, dammit."

"Ruff," Carlos said heavily, "I don't give a damn
about those cattle anymore, about the money, the
rancho—let my uncles have it all."

"I still care, Carlos. I care about the people who
need that damned beef. That's enough conversation.
Get up and get with it!"

Then, without looking back, Ruff Justice went out
into the swirl of rain. The cabin stood directly before
him, dark, solid, aloof, and within it was a beautiful,
terrified woman. And sudden death.

13

The cabin door was heavy, solid. Ruff placed his hand on the damp wood and nudged. It swung open a fraction of an inch. He had had a chance like this once before, a chance to finish Chavez, and he had blown it. This night it would be different. He wouldn't be taken prisoner, he wouldn't be bluffed. Death was coming, hard and fast, violent death, and Justice was the delivery man.

There was no point in hesitating. The longer he remained outside the cabin, the longer he remained visible to any prowling guards.

He sucked it up and shoved on through, closing the door silently behind him. There were six beds, but only three of them were occupied.

He saw movement on the lower bunk near him, saw even in that light the soft curve of shoulder and breast, the dark hair cascading down Elena's back.

"Get dressed, we're going," Ruff said.

"No."

It was Alfredo who had said it. He still hadn't moved. He was on his back in the opposite bunk, and in his hand a Colt revolver gleaming dully in the faint light of the cabin.

"Forget it, Alfredo, I'm leaving."

Chato had risen. Now he slipped to the floor, lazily, catlike as before. "You see, Justice, you are covered. Keep the gun on him, Alfredo. Fire if he moves." Chato came forward a step.

"It won't work. Elena, are you ready? I'm taking

her, and that's that. Alfredo, if you've got any sense, toss the gun away."

"Shoot him, Alfredo," Chato hissed.

"Chato, I—" What was going on in Alfredo's mind was anyone's guess. Maybe he was thinking of the night he had been lying on the hard earth, slowly bleeding to death, and his enemy had cared for him, taken him to María at Zopilote. Maybe he was seeing his brother, knowing that he was mad, knowing that everyone who followed Chato was riding a hard trail to death.

"I can't," he said, lowering his arm.

"Come on, Elena." Ruff turned toward the door and the bandit chief growled. The sound was scarcely human, it rose from deep in his throat, and he lunged toward Alfredo, grabbing for the pistol.

Ruff flung himself through the air across the cabin, dragging Chato down by the heels. It was over that quickly. Chato banged his head hard against the two-by-four rail of the bunk bed and lay still on the floor.

Ruff rose to look into the black eyes of Alfredo Chavez. "Is he dead?" Alfredo asked.

"I don't care enough to find out," Justice told him. "What about you, Alfredo? What do I do about you?"

"I won't do anything—just go," the kid said. His head was hanging as he sat up on his bed, looking at his brother's sprawled, motionless form. "I won't call out."

"If you do, it's the same as killing this woman," Ruff reminded him.

"I said I wouldn't, dammit! I have some honor left. I only curse the day I met you, Ruff Justice. And the day I decided to ride with *him*," he added more quietly.

"Come on," Ruff said to Elena. "Quickly and silently."

"Ruff . . ." She clung to him briefly, and Ruff frowned. It was no time for gratitude.

He opened the door, looking out into the stormy night. By now Carlos and the others should be ready. By now Cosacha should be set to close the gap.

"Stay beside me," Ruff whispered, "and stay low."

They moved then toward the trees surrounding the tents opposite them. The rain and darkness covered their crossing and within minutes Ruff had located the string of horses tied beneath the pines.

"Up," he told Elena, helping her aboard a tall, white-faced bay horse. He slipped the bridle on and gave her the reins. Ruff was aboard a strapping chestnut and now he leaned down to cut the tether that held the other horses. He walked the chestnut into them, nudging horses out of his way as Elena watched. When he had them scattered, he rejoined her.

"At the first gunshot you ride. Just ride like hell, Elena. Through the pass and down that trail as fast and as far as that horse will carry you."

The first shot came a hell of a lot sooner than Ruff had anticipated. He never knew if Alfredo had changed his mind, bowing to some outlaw ethic, or if a roving guard had spotted one of the prisoners, but suddenly the night came alive. The first crackling report rolled across the clearing and Ruff whipped Elena's horse across the flank, seeing it lurch ahead as Elena, her eyes wide, hair flying, clung to its neck.

He watched her as the horse raced out of the woods and across the open ground. Then he drew his handgun and sat for one minute, waiting.

Three more shots were fired across the valley and then a string of them, like hail on a tin roof. The bandits, rousted from their sleep, were rushing toward their horses, some still carrying their boots. Justice had been expecting that, and he calmly shot down the first two bandits, emptying his gun in that direction before he laid heels to that chestnut and it took off like a jackrabbit toward the flat.

At the first shot Carlos, Miguel, and Vargas had done what Ruff had told them to do. Firing their own guns overhead, they had charged at the numbed cattle, startling them into motion. By the time Ruff reached open ground, the thundering of their hooves was rolling through the valley as an all-out stampede rushed toward the pass. Ruff caught a fleeting glimpse of Miguel, saw a bandit rise up before the cattle out of the rainy night and try to halt the herd before he was trampled into the ground by the wild-eyed steers.

Ruff heard the close whiff of a bullet, heard the popping of more distant guns, and then there was only the night and the herd, the blind rush of hundreds of panicked cattle toward the only escape route—the trail that ran between the two upthrust, rocky pinnacles ahead.

Justice could no longer see Elena. She should have been through the pass by now—if she wasn't, there was nothing anyone could do to help her. The skies suddenly opened up again and it began to rain so hard that at first Ruff thought a distant scatter-gun had sprayed him with lead pellets. There was nothing but the incredible roar of the herd, the clapping of thunder, the driving rush of rain.

He could only barely make out the pinnacles now in the murky night. They seemed far distant, miles from him, and then he was through the cut, barely outdistancing the lead steer. Ruff dismounted on the run and scrambled back through the mud and rain, climbing above the herd to a level a dozen shots in the direction of the pursuit.

Anxiously now he looked to the pinnacle, sudden fear striking at his heart. Cosacha should have cut those boulders loose by now.

If he was able to. Justice looked up anxiously, seeing nothing, no one. Perhaps the rocks had simply not given way as Ruff thought they should—or perhaps they had gotten the big Jumano. In that case, they were all done.

Lightning flared against the sky, spitting forked heat through the roiling clouds. Justice saw the last of the herd clear the pass, saw Carlos, riding low over his horse's withers, clutching the pommel for dear life with his good hand. He caught sight of Miguel, circling back, perhaps looking for his *patrón*.

Then, like storm demons rising up out of the ground to strike while the thunder pealed, Ruff saw the mounted Chavez men bearing down on them. Wide-chested horses glossed with rain, dark-slickered men with rifles in hand. The small red winks of muzzle flashes as death sang around Ruff, the ricochets of the bullets, twisted fragments of hot lead singing angrily, audible even above the continuous rumbling of the night skies.

Ruff took aim, saw a man roll with his horse. And then the rumbling grew even louder. Justice glanced up and lit out of there, knowing that it was not thunder, nor the pounding of hooves he heard.

Slowly a cart-sized boulder had begun to roll, slamming into other, smaller rocks, setting them to motion. Then the whole bank began to go. Head-sized boulders bounded high into the air. A great shelf of rock sloughed off, creaking and groaning as gravity stretched out irresistible arms and drew the rock and earth into the pass.

Half a dozen Chavez riders had achieved the pass when the rock began to go. Now they reined back hard, sending frantic horses rearing up on hind legs, their shrill whinnying filling the night, joining the rumbling, sparking, crackling sounds it already made.

Ruff saw a man with a huge mustache, his face white in the glare of lightning, try to turn his horse and be smashed to the ground by tons of crushing stone.

Then he saw nothing else. The crown of the hill

seemed to leap toward the gap below it, a flood of mud and showers of boulders burying the pass.

Ruff stood for a moment, watching the earth settle as the rain fell down in waves before the whipping wind. He stood, arms dangling, exhausted not in body but in spirit, deeply pleased with himself and the ways of the world. He could have fallen down, spent, to sleep in that rain and wind.

"Well?" Cosacha appeared, scrambling down the hill slope. "Did I do it right, Mr. Ruff Justice?" He was grinning excitedly.

"Don't cut it so close next time."

"There will be no next time," Cosacha vowed. "When we have done this, I am going back to Saltillo and raise chickens. I will sit in the sun like an old man. No more fighting, no more excitement. One journey like this one is enough to last me."

Ruff looked back a moment longer, not expecting to see anything, but imprinting it on his memory. There was a savage joy to the victory, and along with it an overwhelming sadness. All those men dead, for what? Ruff felt sadness but not guilt. They had, after all, come looking for what they got. Their entire lives had been a mad rush after judgment, and on this stormy night judgment had fallen.

"Ruff!" Elena was in his arms, her dress rain-heavy, her body warm beneath it. She kissed his face, his neck, clinging to him as Cosacha stood watching, a smile on his lips.

"Did we all make it?" Ruff asked.

"All of us. Even Vargas."

Ruff put his arm around her waist and they walked back through the mud and rain to his horse. There Carlos and Miguel waited. Vargas sat his horse a little apart from the others.

"Free!" It was Carlos who sang the word out. He offered his good hand, his left, to Ruff, who took it.

"We'd better get down off of here," Justice said. "Those cattle will have stopped running by now.

We'll find them ahead of us on the trail, and as weary as they are, we should be able to manage them easily enough. I don't want to lose them now. Not after all of this."

"It is a lost hope," Miguel said, and Ruff turned sharply toward him.

"Why is that, Miguel?"

"Look at us, Ruff Justice. Five beat-up men. Carlos can hardly ride. Four men, then. Four men to herd those cattle? It is not enough."

"It'll be enough," Justice said. "it'll have to be. I'm damned if I'll lose the game now. Not if I have to carry them up on my back."

"You won't," Carlos said quietly. "Miguel is thinking of me, I believe. He would rather take me to a doctor or take me home to bed than have me continue."

Justice, looking at Miguel, knew that Carlos' guess was correct. The old man would do anything for the *patrón*, as he had done whatever Carlos' grandfather had wished.

"We must go on, Miguel," Carlos said, and the old man nodded.

"*Sí, patrón.*"

They mounted then and headed off down the rain-slick trail toward the desert flats beyond. The cattle were found in bunches, standing on the trail or beside it, befuddled by the night's events. There were forty head missing, but there was no time to search for them. Justice wanted to get off that godforsaken mountain and back onto the desert.

The desert, where now there would be water standing in pools, enough to last them to the border. The desert . . . where the Apaches would be waiting yet.

14

They didn't sleep that night. They spent a cold, damp night pushing the remaining cattle down from Comanche Peak, a close bit of work as total darkness fell and the rain continued to fall. They pushed the steers blindly down a hair-raising stretch of trail where the side dropped off five hundred feet or more to the desert floor below, the occasional lightning panicking the wild-eyed steers who were too weary to make an all-out break, but who balked and lowed, halting dead in their tracks or turning savagely to try goring a horse and its master.

Ruff was stiff in every joint, every muscle, his eyes red and gritty, his hands sore from rope and rein, his legs knotted just from sitting that hard, wet saddle.

But dawn broke magnificently, lifting their spirits. The sun blossomed like a deep-red rose through the fleet of scudding, flat-bottomed gray clouds, flushing the desert to crimson, gleaming on the standing pools of water, lying like mirrors scattered across the savage land.

They came down out of the gorge and onto the flats just as the sun rose, and they halted, weary, soaked to the bone, to let the horses breathe while they watched the explosion of color and light to the east.

"Damn me, if it isn't a fine morning to be alive," Ruff Justice said under his breath. Elena was at his side, her cheeks flushed with dawn colors, her dark eyes fresh and alive, looking up into his face.

Deliberately Ruff turned away from her and said aloud, "Two hours. Let's get those saddles off and rub them down. Two hours and we'll start pushing these knock-kneed beggars home."

Elena stood watching, the gleam in her eyes turning to hurt. The tall man walked away from her, leading his recovered white-faced gray. She turned away sharply and stalked to her own horse, seeing Cosacha's look of amusement. She started to lash out at him, held her tongue, and walked on more slowly.

"Are you all right?" she asked Carlos. He was trying to uncinch and was making rough work of it with one hand.

"I couldn't be better," he said, "not on this morning. I feel like king of the world."

"A king without the strength to unsaddle his horse," she said sourly. Her nimble fingers got to work at the cinch and Carlos stood watching her, surprised at the lithe strength of Elena María Cortes as she swung the saddle to the ground in one easy motion.

"Your arm," she said, facing the horse and not Carlos, "will it have to come off?"

"Very likely," he said.

"It is a shame."

"I have grown accustomed to it," Carlos said lightly, "but that is life, no?"

"That is life." She stood staring across the horse's back at the pinkening desert. A nearby clump of mesquite cast lacy shadows on the sand and she watched them for a moment. She turned as she felt a hand on her shoulder.

"You are not so happy this morning, I think," Carlos said.

"Would you be?" she spat out. "To the rest of you a great victory has been won. To me"—she shrugged —"it seems I might as well have stayed with that animal Chavez as face . . ." She spun around and walked away, leaving her sentence unfinished.

Carlos watched her for a long minute, studying

the erect carriage, the proud set of her shoulders, her hair drying in the sunlight, the slight, feminine swing of hips, then he turned with a sigh and started rubbing his horse's back dry.

"Someone coming!" It was Cosacha who roared out the warning, and all work stopped abruptly as rifles were snatched up.

"Where?" Ruff asked, and Cosacha lifted a finger.

There was nothing to see at first, then gradually the dark mass moved out of the background of clouds and sun and took on form.

Justice felt his hand tense on his rifle, felt his mouth set tightly. "No more," he heard Elena say desperately, "God let there be no more of this fighting."

"Federales!" Cosacha's joyous cry filled the air. He broke into a little jig step, throwing his arms out wildly. "By God, Justice, I never thought I would see the time when Cosacha, the Jumano Indian, would feel joy at the sight of these brown-uniformed dogs. Now I would kiss their feet."

Justice wasn't prepared to go that far, but he knew what Cosacha meant. As they watched the line of mounted soldiers approach, he felt as if a weight had been lifted from his shoulders.

"Soldiers, so what?" Vargas said acidly.

"So what?" Cosacha said. "I'll tell you so what, *amigo*. The Federales are in the area. The Apaches will scuttle to their holes. Do you think that we were through with Chavez, too? I do not think so. They would come after us, those that are alive, if for no reason but revenge. Now there will be no more Chavez men, my friend, Vargas. Thanks to the Federales."

In fifteen minutes the federal officers had arrived at their camp. A stiff-necked captain named Hernández, who conducted the entire interview from horseback, took the story from Carlos.

"They are up there yet?" he asked, his eyes lifting to the gaunt, red Comanche Peak.

"Yes, Captain, they must be. There is no way out."

"There is no way now. I've been hunting that murderous bastard for six months. Now I shall have him. I only hope none of them surrender," he said malignantly.

"You don't have to worry about that," Ruff Justice said, and the captain shot him a searching glance.

"Is there a possibility," Carlos asked, "that you could spare some of your men to escort our party to the border? As you see, we are few and we have a woman with us."

"That is impossible," the captain said. "I wish you luck, but I have other uses for my people. *Vayan con Dios.*" He touched the brim of his cap to Elena, lifted his hand, and then led out, the men following in Hernández' wake.

Justice stood watching them, then he shook his head and turned away. "I notice you didn't try kissing his boot," he said to Cosacha.

"That pig! But still, Justice, we have finally run out of our bad luck. The trail now should be clear to the border. With luck, two days and we are there, the army pens filled with beef, my pockets filled with silver, my stomach with mescal if you uncivilized *norteamericanos* have such a thing."

"I'll find you some," Ruff promised. "Failing that, I'll promise you a good substitute."

Ruff finished rubbing down his gray and then sat in the horse's shade, watching the milling herd, hoping that what Cosacha had said was true, that they had at last run out of bad luck.

Before they had broken camp, they began hearing the shooting from the mountains. Hernández had found his quarry and Ruff didn't think there would be any surrendering—not officially. He shook his head, thinking about Alfredo Chavez, a kid who had just started down the wrong path and kept going. Sometimes it's too late to change, even when common sense tells a man he has to. It was too late now for Alfredo.

By noon they were moving again. Across the cloud-shadowed desert the herd ambled on, every rider working hard to keep them moving.

There was water everywhere, although the thirsty sands were rapidly drinking it up. They camped at dusk beside a silver pond nearly an acre across. There were gray willows growing alongside the pond, and dead in the center of it an ancient cottonwood, only its withered head showing.

Vargas was watering his horse when Ruff came up to him, leading the gray, squinting into the glare the late sun cast on the pond.

"Sticking to the bitter end, are you?" Ruff said.

Vargas turned slowly, his expression unreadable. "Why not? Where would I go now?"

"Sonorita? To your cousin."

"I have changed my mind about that. Besides"—he shrugged—"the desert is unsafe for a man alone."

"It hasn't exactly been a picnic with all of us together."

"No." Vargas laughed. "A long trail, no? Maybe I just want to see this herd delivered now. It's as if I have a stake in it, too, after all we've been through."

"Is that it?" Ruff asked.

"What else?" Vargas shrugged.

"I don't know. It's just that it's most unlikely, the tale you tell. A man would think that you had other business than you've revealed."

"Would he?" Vargas lifted his shoulders again. "Why is that, Mr. Justice?"

"I was just thinking back . . ." Ruff's gray swung its head around and nudged him with its wet muzzle, and Ruff pushed the horse away. "The night you rode in. Here we are in Mexico and yet you come riding in hailing the camp in English."

"So?"

"Kind of odd, don't you think? Why would you

believe there were English-speaking men in that camp?"

"It was only a hunch, a sort of knowledge I can't explain—I've always had this sixth sense about me," Vargas said, and Ruff was surprised that he could say it with a straight face.

"No, you had to know. That meant you've known all along exactly what you were doing, and that wasn't riding to some cousin's house in Sonorita, it was tagging along with this herd for a purpose I can't guess."

"But you have been guessing," Vargas said.

"I have been. Tell me, did you know Elena Cortes before?"

"No."

"You're sure."

"I said so. What is your idea, Justice? Do you think I'm a rejected suitor, a lover trailing along after Elena to make sure she does not marry this Will Dobbs?"

"It occurred to me."

Then, disarmingly, Vargas laughed again. "She pays me much attention, no?"

"Maybe that was it. Maybe she paid you no attention whatsoever and it annoyed you. Maybe it annoyed you enough to take a shot at a man who was getting some attention from Elena Cortes."

"You?"

"Know of anyone else who's nearly been murdered?"

"It is absurd. I swear this to you—I know who the woman is, but I am not infatuated with her. I did not try to kill you for that reason or for any other reason."

And Justice believed him. "But you won't tell me why you're here, Vargas."

"I am a wanderer," he said, smiling so that his teeth flashed out of the shadow of his hat brim.

Ruff just looked at him. Then, knowing he wasn't going to get anything else out of the man, he turned and walked away, leading the gray.

The campfire glowed dully. Ruff walked to the fire, seeing Carlos lying down, eyes open, looking like death warmed over.

"How's the arm?"

"Not good. There is a surgeon at Fort Sumner?"

"One of the best. He'll patch you together right enough. Probably won't even be any stiffness."

"No," Carlos said, "I do not think there will be any stiffness when the surgeon is finished."

"Don't get your mind made up that it's coming off. You're not a doctor and neither am I."

"That is true," Carlos said, but his expression didn't hold much hope.

Miguel had returned and the old man squatted down beside Carlos to give him water and tug his blanket up. Ruff walked slowly away. Cosacha was out riding guard; Justice would relieve him at midnight.

The desert night was soft, deep purple, and along the edge of the pond toads had started to croak. There would be plenty of them hatching out with this rain. Odd creatures, these desert toads would lie dormant beneath the sand for months, even years, waiting for the rains to come. Now the rain had come, and they would live briefly, mating to produce more toads, which would lie beneath the baked earth waiting for another storm.

"I saw you speaking to Vargas. What did he say?"

Elena had come up beside Ruff. Now she clung to his arm, leaning her head against his shoulder as they stood watching the shimmer of the pond, the stars beginning to blink on above the desert.

"He knows nothing, tells nothing," Ruff said. "Elena, have you met him before?"

"No. Why?"

"Because I don't understand Vargas, I don't know what he's after."

"Don't worry about that. He is not a violent man."

"Someone is. Someone tried to kill me."

"Pablo. It was Pablo, and now he is gone."

"Maybe. It seemed abrupt even for the pup. You never gave him any encouragement, did you?"

Elena stiffened momentarily, drawing away from Ruff a bare inch. "Certainly not," she said, fighting back her anger.

"It's over you, Elena, I know it is."

"Do you think so?" Her hand had slipped onto Ruff's chest and she was facing him, her eyes lighted by the stars. "Shall we give him another chance, then, Ruff, another reason for wanting you dead."

He kissed her, drawing her to him, feeling her breasts against him, the slow joining of their bellies, the warm, parting lips of Elena Cortes.

"No," he said, holding her shoulders, looking into her eyes, "we won't give him another reason."

"Justice, I need you. By tomorrow—tomorrow my life will begin to end. The fat Texan will come for me and it will be over." Her hands gripped his shirt-front with a sort of frenzy. "I need you tonight," she said in a taut whisper.

"Not tonight," Ruff said, and he saw her eyes go cold, saw her mouth set harshly, felt her hands drop away from his shoulders.

"You are so afraid someone will kill you?" she asked scornfully.

"It's not that."

"It is not that," she repeated, shaking her head. "It is that I am not exciting to you. You do not wish to be bothered. You go to hell, Ruff Justice! You go straight to your hell."

Then she stalked away, her arms folded under her breasts, her back rigid, and Ruff watched her go, finding her so damned exciting, wanting her so much that he nearly called her back. But he didn't. He turned away himself, taking slow deep breaths as he walked to the pond, crouched down, and sat motionless for a long while, listening to the dry croaking of the toads.

Ruff rose with the dawn after a sleepless night. Miguel, who had had the last watch, roused him from his blanket as the sun, a great glowing red ball, began to peer over the horizon. Feeling dry, brittle, angry, Justice rose and began saddling his horse, his belly complaining continuously. Hungry, tired, sore, Ruff only wanted this trek over with. The savage joy of the day before was completely gone. Gone with Elena's love.

There had been no other choice about that, none at all; maybe later she would understand his reasons.

"Ready?" Cosacha looked healthy, happy. His powerful body had mended itself faster than anyone had believed possible. There were only the faint purple splotches around his eyes to give witness to the terrible beatings he had taken.

"I'm ready, get them moving. I'm sick of this desert, sick of Mexico."

"Ah, I see," Cosacha said, and damn him, he was grinning. He turned his horse and walked it to the far side of the herd, Ruff still grumbling as he swung into leather.

Ruff rode at the point. Miguel and Vargas had the flanks. Cosacha was at drag with Carlos, who couldn't do a whole lot. He was wobbly in the saddle now, riding hunched forward, his mouth drawn down with agony. Elena rode beside him, probably because it was as far as she could get from Ruff Justice. He had passed her earlier in the morning and she had looked right through him.

They were into dune country now, the sand rising and falling softly, in wind-contoured hills. They were also into the United States, and that alone seemed to brighten Ruff's attitude.

They labored through the dunes for most of the day, the cattle at times needing help as they sank to their bellies in the soft sand. By late afternoon they had eased onto the grasslands north of Arroyo

Grande. A good marksman with a good rifle could have hit the fort with a bullet.

The fort. Warm food and a bed, drink, and safety. Justice anticipated it gloomily. He was suddenly tired of New Mexico Territory, its dust and heat. He longed for the high mountains, the long ranks of pines stirring in the cool breeze.

The long line of armed men appeared off the plains, bearing down on the herd. Justice yanked his rifle free of the saddle boot and raised a hand in signal.

Vargas was coming at a dead run, Miguel, with Cosacha, trailing.

"What is it?" Vargas asked breathlessly. "Soldiers?"

"No, I'm afraid not," Justice answered. "It's a man named Dunweather. Kyle Dunweather."

15

"What is happening?" Cosacha asked, settling his sweaty horse. "Who is that, Ruff Justice?"

"The man who will do anything to stop this herd from getting through to the fort, my friend. Kyle Dunweather, who makes a living selling short, selling sick cattle to the army and the Indian agency. These cattle spell ruin to him. If it can be done once, it can be done again. Another herd and another can be driven up to feed the army if necessary. Dunweather knows this. He followed me to Corbett City and tried to have me killed. He didn't bother following me into Mexico—too much risk there. Besides, all he had to do was wait. I'd have to come back this way, and when I did, he'd be ready."

Cosacha had been unlimbering his weapons as Ruff talked. The rancher and his men were nearer now, appearing as a long mounted picket line on the desert. Dark shadows more than men, but each shadow was carrying a deadly weapon.

"What do we do?" Cosacha asked tightly.

"Keep the herd moving. Slowly. At the first shot, start them to running, and you scatter—all of you—I won't see anyone die after all we've been through."

"But you—" Justice had started his horse forward and Cosacha laid a hand on his bridle. "What are you doing, *hombre*?"

"I'm going to have a talk with the man."

"Then I am coming."

"The hell you are. Stay put. I told you what to do."

"I resign," Cosacha said, and he was grinning. "I quit this job—it is too hard and the pay too low. I do not work for you, Ruff Justice. Now, then, try to keep me from going. Without killing me," he added.

"All right, if it's got to be that way. Miguel, you heard what I told Cosacha?"

"I heard you, Mr. Ruff Justice."

"I mean it—I don't want you dying for this herd."

"No more than you," Miguel said, and Ruff saw that he was going to have a hard time of it. These people had fought Apaches and bandits, hard weather and hard country for this herd. They weren't going to be backed off now. Not by the likes of Kyle Dunweather.

"Come on," Justice grumbled, heeling his gray forward, his rifle loose in his right hand. Cosacha was at his side like a massive shadow.

Their horses' hooves whispered through the dry grass. Somewhere down in a draw a quail called hauntingly. Kyle Dunweather had halted his men and they sat motionless against the plain, watching as Ruff approached them.

Now Ruff could make out the cattleman's face, dry, pinched. His scraggly red beard was drifting in the wind. Beside him sat a taller, younger man with the same stamp on him. The others seemed to be ordinary cowhands, men working for a crooked brand. They would fight for that brand with their peculiar loyalty, and maybe they would die for it, all so that Kyle Dunweather could grow fatter while a reservation full of Indians were poisoned by bad beef.

Justice slowed his gray to a walk, approaching Dunweather slowly, eyes alert for any motion. Mentally he counted the men—sixteen of them, far too many to have any hope of defeating in an out-and-out battle.

Dunweather watched them, his colorless eyes bleak and empty.

Ruff halted his horse in front of the cattleman and said, "Was there something you wanted?"

"You're Ruff Justice?"

"That's right."

"Then what I want," Dunweather drawled, "is for you to turn them cattle around and get your butt back into Mexico."

"A man doesn't always get what he wants, Dunweather," Justice replied. "Sometimes he just doesn't get his way."

"Like now?"

"That's what I'm trying to convey."

"You going to outshoot us?" Dunweather asked, his lips parting in a yellow-toothed smile.

"No, I guess not. I'll tell you this, however; you'll damn sure be the first to go if the shooting starts. Do you understand that, Dunweather? You'll be the first. One of us will get you. I don't know what you hope to gain here, exactly, but you don't win much of a victory if you have to die to prove your point, do you?"

The kid next to Dunweather guffawed loudly. "He acts like we ought to be afraid of *them*!"

"That your kid, Dunweather?"

"He is. That's my son."

"He's the second one to go. Hear that, Cosacha? If anyone starts shooting, I'll take Dunweather, you take his wise-ass kid."

"I understand, Ruff Justice."

Suddenly the kid wasn't laughing anymore.

"He doesn't miss," Ruff added for good measure.

"You can't bluff me, Justice," Dunweather said, heating up. "I've faced men like you before, back in Texas. Men who wanted what was mine. My house, my land, my cattle. They tried to take it from me too, but damn me, they couldn't do it. A bunch of goddamned outlaws was all the carpetbaggers were. Plain thieves."

"And what do you call this, Dunweather?" Ruff

asked, letting his eyes shift to the cowhands', to meet their gaze one by one. "If this isn't plain thieving, I don't know what you call it."

"I've got the government contract! The only cattle they can legally buy are mine. You're trying to undercut me, Justice—you're the one who's in the wrong."

"Am I?" Ruff was speaking to the cowboys now, ignoring Dunweather. "Men, you might feel you have to fight Dunweather's war for him. Maybe you're afraid of losing your jobs. I'll tell you this—you won't have a job anyway after this day's work is done, if you follow Dunweather. You won't have anything but a price on your head—those of you who live through it. These are United States army cows, friends. You take them, you'll have to kill us; you kill us and you'll hang, believe me. Every soldier from here to California will be on the lookout for you."

"Shut up, Justice," Dunweather growled. "My men know the truth of things."

"If they do, then they know they're in the wrong! They know that the reason these cattle had to be brought up is because you've been cheating the army. That's right, cheating them. Lining your pocket at their expense, at the expense of the reservation Indians who've been sold infected beef. Those Indians aren't going to take any more, Dunweather. They'll break off that reservation if they don't get the beef rations they've been promised, and when that happens, this country is going to run with blood. All because you have to have it your way, right or wrong making no difference. Your way, and the rest of civilization be damned!"

"Are you finished?" Dunweather asked coldly.

"Yes, I guess so." Ruff looked up and down the rank of cowhands. "You men know who's telling you the truth here. Do what you have to do, but it seems to me there's a few things worth more than a month's wages. Those cattle down there are for the soldiers at Fort Sumner and for the reservation Indians. That's who you're robbing. But you'll have to fight for them. I'll tell you all about my army. There's me and the Indian here. Then we've got a man close on to seventy years old, a kid with a smashed-up arm, and a woman. But they won't surrender the herd. They as much as told me that. So you'll have to kill them. If you can stomach killing the old, the crippled, and a woman for a cause you should damn well know is wrong, then do it. Let's do it now."

"He's right, you know," said a man with a brown mustache and a heavy Texas drawl. "I'm pulling off. Ed, how about you and me seeing Colorado?"

"Damn you, MacCaffiter," Dunweather shouted, "you'd turn coat on me after all we've been through!"

"I'd have to, Mr. Dunweather," the Texan replied, "I don't favor whiskers."

"What in the hell are you talking about?"

"I reckon I'd have to grow a beard, Mr. Dunweather—I sure as hell couldn't look at myself in a shaving mirror again. Not if I went through with what you're intendin'." He turned again to his partner. "Ed? Let's mosey."

"Need company?" a third man asked.

"We can stand it," MacCaffiter said, and the three men pulled out of the line, Dunweather's eyes clawing at them.

"Damn you, Justice," the rancher said, "I ought to kill you with my bare hands."

"Would you like the chance?" Before Dunweather could answer or understand what was happening, Justice had slipped from the saddle, tossing his rifle to Cosacha, who sat impassively watching. In two strides Justice was to Dunweather, and reaching up, he grabbed Dunweather by the belt and hauled him out of the saddle.

The big cattleman hit the ground hard. Ruff Justice was over him, fists bunched angrily.

"Here it is, Dunweather," Justice growled. "Here's your chance to teach me a lesson with your two hands. That's the trouble with you, you keep letting other men do your fighting for you. Like those clowns in Corbett City. Now let's see what you can do on your own. Get up on your hind legs, Dunweather, and let's see what kind of man you really are."

"Don't do it, Pa," the kid shouted, but Dunweather had to fight and he knew it. To back down in front of his men was unthinkable. Slowly he rose, eyes on Ruff.

There was hatred in those eyes, bitter hatred. He was in this to the finish, and if he had the chance to kill, he would gladly kill Justice.

"Come on, Pa," the punk said.

"Gouge him, Mr. Dunweather."

Justice backed away in a crouch, slowly circling as Dunweather came in, his hands low, savage eyes gleaming. "I'll have you, Justice."

"Get to it, then, Dunweather. You always prove your point by talking?" Justice taunted him. "Come on, let's see what you can do by yourself, without twenty gunmen at your side."

With a roar Dunweather lunged. It was a wild, clumsy move made out of frustration and rage. Justice stepped back, stuck out a foot, and Dunweather tripped over it and went down flat on his face.

When he rose, there was blood on his face. Blood and dust. His lip trembled like a small child's. He dusted himself and came at Ruff again, circling the lanky, buckskin-clad man warily.

Ruff had been standing loosely, hands at his waist. Now as he saw an opening, his left hand flicked out, stabbing Dunweather twice in the face, rocking his head back as Ruff's jab snapped against it.

Dunweather tried to grab Ruff's wrist, missed, and took another sharp jab. The cattleman stepped back, wiping the hair from his eyes.

"Take him, Pa," the punk shrilled.

Dunweather came in flat-footed this time, his shoulders hunched forward, chin tucked in. He leaped at the tall man and felt his shoulder collide with Ruff's chest. They went down together, Dunweather flailing away with both arms, trying to destroy Justice.

Ruff took a shot to the rib cage, another to the jaw. Then he slammed his knee up hard between Dunweather's legs and the cattleman went slack. Ruff shoved him aside and tried to get to his feet.

Dunweather reached out and hooked Ruff's wrist, dragging him down. More quickly than Ruff would have thought possible, the rancher was up, and as he achieved his feet, he began battering away at Ruff with his boot. The first kick knocked the wind from Ruff and lit his skull with little silver-and-gold pinwheels. He rolled away, catching a glancing kick on the skull.

Justice came to his feet, stabbing out with that left hand. Dunweather, more confident now, came in on him. It was a mistake.

Justice let a right-hand shot go from low down. It arced up and caught Dunweather on the eye, splitting the hide over the cheekbone. Blood began to flow profusely and Dunweather cursed under his breath; reacting furiously, he started throwing lefts and rights from everywhere.

Ruff blocked or ducked under most of them, but a looping uppercut got through, landing on the point of Ruff's jaw. He staggered backward, hearing a cheer go up as Dunweather followed with a left that landed flush on the cheek.

Dunweather kicked out, trying to break Ruff's knee-cap with his heavy boot heel, but Justice managed to twist away, catching a painful but less damaging kick on the shins. Ruff was still backing away and now he felt himself up against a horse. There was a Dunweather rider above him and the cowboy reached down and took a handful of Ruff's hair in his hand, holding him tightly as Dunweather plodded in, throwing two hard body blows, the second of which landed with stunning pain on Ruff's liver.

Justice kicked out at Dunweather and simultaneously reached up, scratching at the arm of the mounted cowhand, trying to find a grip.

What he found was fingers. The fingers wound into his hair, and fending Dunweather off with another kick, Ruff took the cowboy's thumb and bent back savagely until the sickening crack of bone, the cry of pain, sounded.

Shaking free, Justice went after Dunweather. Two lefts, then a right backed the rancher off. Ruff went in close and started working to the belly, his forehead buried in the hollow of the rancher's shoulder.

Dunweather's hands found Ruff's face and his thumbs started digging for the eyes. Ruff shook his head, fighting off the clawing gouge. Dunweather was panting hard now. His face was crimson with exertion.

But he was far from through. The rancher hammered down at Ruff's face with his thick-knuckled fists, trying to drive Justice into the ground. Justice grunted with the pain as a stunning right clipped his ear and landed with force on the base of his neck.

Justice ducked his head and then brought it up. His skull crashed into the rancher's jaw and blood spewed out, soaking them both as the tip of Dunweather's tongue was severed by violently meeting teeth.

Dunweather put up a protective hand and Justice slapped it away, driving a right into Dunweather's nose. Again the blood gushed forth. Dunweather was backing up now, his punches growing weak and infrequent. Still the kid was screaming.

"Kill him, Pa! Kill him!"

Dunweather didn't look to be doing anything like that now. His heart was gone, and although he still fought back as Justice waded in, there was no sting to the blows, no anger, no hatred, no weight of leg and shoulder, chest and haunch. They were feeble waves and Justice, feeling no mercy for the man, kept coming.

Dunweather caught a chopping hook on the jaw and went to his knees. Justice backed away, his chest rising and falling raggedly, his hair hanging in his eyes, his fists clenched.

"Get up," Justice commanded, and Dunweather obeyed. He rose and Justice hit him again. This time a left that had all of Ruff's weight behind it. It landed on Dunweather's already-damaged nose, splitting it, bringing more blood.

Dunweather went down again.

"Get up, damn you," Justice panted, stepping back. "Get up, Dunweather."

And he tried. Ruff had to give him that. He tried to get up. He got to his knees and then to one foot before he sagged back to the ground to kneel there, head hanging. When he looked up again, there were tears streaming from his eyes. The tears of a child. He tried to say something, but it was only a sobbing little squeak when it came out.

"We're coming through you," Ruff said. Then he turned and walked away, his knees more shaky than he would have wanted anyone to know.

The close roar of a muzzle blast jerked Ruff's head around. He had filled his hand with his Colt and gone to one knee before he saw that it was over.

Dunweather's son was sitting his horse, a pistol dangling from his hand. As Justice watched, the kid nodded and slumped from the saddle to the ground, to lie there groaning.

Justice's eyes flickered to the side and he saw the smoke still curling from the muzzle of Cosacha's rifle.

"You see, Ruff Justice, sometimes a man needs help," the Indian said, and Ruff nodded his thanks.

Dunweather had crawled and staggered to where his son lay bleeding from the shoulder. Now he knelt there, blood and tears washing down his face.

"Well?" Justice asked at length. He looked at the other cowhands. "There's Colorado or there's hell."

"Believe the cooler climates suit me," one man cracked.

"I never thought the kid would go to backshooting." He looked at the injured punk and at his father, broken, destroyed. "Hell, I couldn't fight for them nohow—even if they was right."

"We got no fight, Justice. If you'll allow, we're pulling out now. Slowly," he said with a grin. Then they turned their horses and walked them away, the skies going deep purple overhead, the wind rising, cool against Ruff's perspiration-soaked body.

"And now?" Cosacha asked. The wind lifted his horse's mane and flattened the grass. The dark eyes looked out of the bruised face at Ruff Justice. He tucked his rifle away in the saddle boot.

"Now," Ruff Justice said, "we take those cattle home and be damned to them all."

Then, grinning at Cosacha, he swung up onto the gray and together they rode back across the purpling land toward the herd, where Miguel and Vargas sat side by side watching, where Elena waited with Carlos Trujillo.

"It is over?" Carlos asked, and Justice told him.

"It's over."

Over but for one thing. There was someone riding with this herd who had come in the night trying to murder Ruff Justice, and Justice knew who it was. The drive was over, the cattle had come home. But there was still that little matter to be finished.

"Shall I take the point?" Vargas asked.

"Yes." Justice sat looking at the two men ahead of them. An old man and his wounded son. Dunweather got the kid onto his horse and then mounted stiffly himself. Justice let the Dunweathers ride out of sight before he lifted his voice and called out, "Let's get them home to bed!"

16

"Damn you, Ruff Justice!" The colonel popped up from behind his desk, his face glowing, his grin lifting his ears, cutting wrinkles into the skin around his eyes. "You made it! I'll be damned." The colonel crossed the room and shook hands with the scout, who, he noticed, looked dusty, weary, bloody, and gaunt.

"We did make it, sir, and happy to be back."

"Trouble?" the colonel asked.

"Some."

"Dunweather didn't try to stop you, did he?"

"Who?"

"All right," the colonel said, laughing, "you don't have to give me the details. Where's the owner of the herd?"

"He's at the surgeon's right now. He's going to lose an arm."

"Too bad." The colonel leaned back in his chair. Ruff, propped up loosely in his, seemed on the verge of falling asleep. "I've got payment in gold for the man. We can count tomorrow and get the cattle on their way to the agency."

"Fine," Ruff said lazily. The warm, familiar office seemed to be filling with a haze. The room swayed gently from side to side, lulling him to sleep.

"For God's sake, go on over and find a bunk for yourself. You've a woman with you? We'll find a cottage for her. She can be in with Mrs. Davitts. She must be the one this Dobbs has been waiting for. William Dobbs—know him?"

"Heard of him," Ruff said. His chin had sunk to his chest. It came up as the colonel placed a hand on his shoulder.

"Get out of here, will you?" he said with genuine fondness. "Get some sleep. Tomorrow's time enough to finish everything up."

Ruff made it to his feet and out of the office. Miguel, Vargas, and Cosacha were waiting in the orderly room and Justice yawned. "Sleep, men. Let's get some sleep."

They went out into the cool, crisp evening. Ruff glanced at the brilliant stars above, at the comfortable sight of a guard walking his post on the parapet. Then they went to the enlisted men's barracks, where bunks were found for them.

There was a card game going on and a soldier playing a mouth harp. It didn't disturb Ruff in the least. When his head touched that pillow, he went out like a light, falling into dreamless, leaden sleep.

At reveille he awoke refreshed, feeling only a lingering stiffness as he sat up, his arms folded between his legs, his head hanging.

Cosacha was still there, but the others had gone.

"To the mess hall," the Jumano said.

Ruff had almost forgotten the last time he had a full meal. "I've got to clean up, Cosacha, I can't stand myself. Go on ahead if you want."

But the Indian elected to wait. Ruff stripped to the waist and scrubbed himself with harsh, yellow lye soap, rinsing off and toweling down briskly. Then he shaved, working carefully around the mustache. That done, he felt human enough to face the world.

He dressed again, promising himself a long, leisurely bath later. Then, brushing his hair back, he nodded to Cosacha and they went out, crossing the parade ground, where soldiers stood in formation for roll call. Justice waved to a man he knew and led Cosacha on toward the mess hall.

Ruff was hungry enough to eat the table, but Cosacha showed him something. Five eggs and a mountain of potatoes, three slices of ham, four cups of coffee, and half a dozen slices of toast with jelly.

"Now," Cosacha said, leaning back, "I can face the world. I need only three things to complete this day. One, my pay from Mr. Ruff Justice; two, a great, terrible bottle of mescal; three, a woman!"

"I can help you with the first two," Ruff said. "As soon as they count those cattle and pay Carlos, I'll give you your money."

"All right. I will be patient, then, Ruff Justice. I tell you this, though—do not be surprised if Cosacha the Jumano is never seen again after today. I am going to hide myself in mescal and in love until I have no more money and no memory of who I am."

They each had one more cup of coffee and then headed off toward the cattle pens. The colonel was already there and Miguel and Vargas had joined him. Hanging around on the fringe of the group was a stout man in a brown twill suit and wide white hat.

"Dobbs?" Ruff asked the colonel.

"No other. Mr. Dobbs is itchy. He's expecting a wife and she hasn't shown."

"No?" Ruff smiled to himself. "Ready to count 'em?" he asked.

"We are. Carlos is still at the surgeon's. The arm came off yesterday. He seems to be doing all right," Hollingshead told him.

"I'll stop by right after this."

"Miguel is going to receive payment—that's all right, isn't it?"

"Of course," Justice said. The world would end before Miguel would think of cheating Rancho Trujillo.

They got to it, then, running the cattle one by one

through a chute, a soldier with a mop and a bucket of red paint daubing the flank of each steer as it was counted. The Indian agent and two of his charges—both Apaches—had arrived, and the three of them watched the proceedings with satisfaction.

When they were finished there, they all walked back to the colonel's office, where Miguel was paid in gold from Hollingshead's strongbox.

"And now," Vargas said, stepping forward. "If you will, Miguel, three thousand pesos are due and payable on the sale."

Miguel, his eyes narrowing, turned toward Vargas, who was smiling.

"Just who are you to ask for such a sum?" Miguel demanded.

"Pardon me." Vargas undid his belt and from a slit in the stitching drew forth his credentials. "I am the assistant tax collector for the Saltillo district."

Miguel looked at the paper and then handed it to Justice, who only shrugged.

"For that you went through what we went through?" Cosacha asked in amazement. "For collecting taxes on a cattle sale?"

"It is my occupation, *señor*." Vargas shrugged. "My commissioner was afraid that payment might not be made on a sale consummated in the United States. He ordered me to go along, and I have done so."

Miguel, after some discussion, paid Vargas and received a receipt for the money. Vargas touched his hat brim and went away satisfied.

William Dobbs was far from satisfied. He burst into the colonel's office five minutes later, demanding to see Elena. "I can't wait around here all week, Colonel. Dammit, I've got business to see to."

"She was not in the cottage?"

"No, she wasn't! Frankly I don't think she's on this post at all. I think someone's flimflamming me."

Ruff Justice spoke up. "I think I can find her, Mr. Dobbs."

"If you can, I'd be much obliged. Tell that young woman that I'll wait exactly one more hour. Then I've got to get down to the stage station and catch me an eastbound."

"I'll tell her," Ruff promised. Miguel shot him a withering glance, which Justice ignored. With Miguel and Cosacha he then walked over to the surgeon's. The doctor was a little man with spectacles who didn't think much of his patient having so many visitors, but he finally agreed to let them go in for a few minutes.

Elena was beside the bed, holding Carlos' hand. He was conscious, but his face seemed drained of blood. The doctor had pumped him full of morphine, but he was still in pain.

"Hello, Carlos," Justice said. "Going to make it?"

"The cattle . . . ?"

"All taken care of. Miguel's got the money. I guess that solves everything, doesn't it?"

Ruff pulled up a chair and sat down next to Carlos' bed, across from Elena, who cast him a scathing glance.

"What do you mean?" Carlos asked through dry lips.

"I mean, now you can marry Elena. That's what you wanted all along, wasn't it? You always loved her, but with the money troubles you had yourself, knowing that she needed money, you were just too damned noble—and foolish—to ask. Hell, Carlos, you two belong together. Both of you young, living side by side down in Mexico . . . You do love her, right?"

"Yes." He looked at Elena and Ruff saw her cheeks flush with joy. "But how did you know, Ruff? I denied it when you asked me."

"I knew when someone started pumping my bed full of bullets, Carlos."

"Not I, Ruff . . . I would never . . ."

"No, I know it. Not you. It was Miguel." Ruff

turned his eyes to the old Mexican. "Wasn't it, Miguel? Miguel, who knew his young *patrón* loved the beautiful woman. Miguel, who would do anything for you, Carlos. When he saw me with Elena, he decided to take things into his own hands."

"Miguel?" Carlos asked. The Mexican just hung his head. He didn't need to answer.

There was a rap at the door and the doctor came in. "Please, you must all leave now. Mr. Trujillo must rest."

Carlos lifted his hand and Ruff took it. Then, with a wink, Justice turned and went out into the sunlight with Miguel, Cosacha, and Elena.

"There's a man waiting for you, Elena. A man named Dobbs, I believe. He says to tell you you've got exactly one hour if you want to be Mrs. Dobbs. I thought maybe you'd like to go over and give him your answer to that personally."

"I would like nothing better," Elena said, her eyes sparking dangerously. Then she turned, threw her arms around Ruff's neck, and kissed him for the last time. "Thank you," she whispered, and then she was off for the colonel's office, Miguel walking with her.

"Well?" Cosacha asked as they stood looking out over the parade ground. "It will be a hell of a time, Justice. I am going to get drunk, fight with every ugly bastard I see, and then find a woman. Will you come with me?"

"No. Thanks, Cosacha, but no. What will you do after the money's gone?"

"Go home. I think maybe some time I will ride over to Rancho Trujillo and see if they have a permanent job for an old Jumano Indian." Cosacha was silent for a while, his eyes looking toward the far places. Then he shook off his pensive mood, grinned, and said, "If you change your mind, Ruff Justice, come and find me in the town. Just go to where there is the most noise and you hear a woman shriek with delight."

He slapped Justice on the shoulder then and shuffled off onto the sunlit parade ground, walking toward the open main gate of Fort Sumner, New Mexico Territory.

The tall man dressed in buckskins stood in the shade of the awning watching him go. Then a roar of surprised pain from the colonel's office brought Ruff's head around, and he started walking that way to see just how far a Texan could bounce.

Echoes of the massacre at Paley Wells rode with
the cavalry contingent. It was a sight not easily
forgotten, though Captain Hart's men had seen much
savagery on the Dakota plains. The Paley family was
gone. The old man, his wife, a teenage son, and a
young daughter. They had been hacked to pieces,
kept alive for too long. Their ghosts would haunt
these plains for a long while to come.

It was Stone Hand who had done it, that was what
Ruffin T. Justice, the tall, buckskinned, flamboyant
civilian scout, had said. He had left his mark on the
bodies.

Stone Hand was Teton Lakota. He was crazy, blood
crazy.

"What sticks in their mind is the meal," Captain
Hart said. He removed his hat and wiped out the
band. The morning breeze was cool across the long
grass valley.

"I know it," Ruff answered.

It was the meal which stuck in Ruff's mind also.
Four Sioux had ridden up to the house and swung
down. Paley and his wife had set the table for four

extra. Then Stone Hand and his men had sat down to eat the Paleys' food, rising to slaughter them after the meal was over.

"I'm going out ahead," Ruff said. The captain nodded, watching the tall, lean man heel his gray and move out. Justice's long dark hair curled down past his shoulders, and it moved in the wind as he rode. He wore a mustache which fell to his jawline, was habitually clad in buckskins. He carried a Colt sidearm, a bowie riding at the back of his belt, and a buckskin-sheathed .56 Spencer carbine that he carried across the saddlebows.

And in his heart he was carrying a deep, dark anger.

He had met Stone Hand before and liked none of what he had learned about the man. Stone Hand's own people had kicked him out of the tribe, disgusted with his barbarism, which could be directed at any human or animal. There was a rumor that Crazy Horse had put a price of fifty ponies on Stone Hand's scalp, but that might or might not have been true.

Ahead lay the pine-stippled foothills north of the Red River. The grass began to give out and the trail which Ruff had been following at an easy canter to dry up.

For the first time that day he swung down and crouched, searching for signs. He led the gray forward a little way, swung left, and picked up the tracks again. Four unshod Indian ponies, two bigger horses taken from the Paley place.

Ruff glanced back, saw the blue-clad file of soldiers a quarter of a mile off, and swung up into leather again. He moved toward the low hills to his right. The tall pines swayed in the wind. The sky was a long-running thing streaked with pale pennants of cloud. A dozen crows wheeled and cawed in the air.

The first shot sang off the cantle of Ruff's saddle and he dropped far to the side of his horse, yelling savagely to get the gray running, running into the timber, as a dozen more shots echoed down the hillslope. Behind him the bugler sounded charge, and although Hart was still far behind, the cavalry kicked itself into a thundering gallop.

The Indians had position, and three of Hart's men went down in the first fusillade. Ruff was into the timber now, and he leaped from the gray, unsheathing the big Spencer as he dropped to the pine needle-covered earth. A bullet tore a chunk of bark from a tree near his right hand and Ruff went to the ground.

His eyes narrowed as he looked upslope to his left, where the shots had come from. Glancing back, he saw that Hart had wisely broken off his wild assault and was regrouping out of rifle range.

That left Ruff alone and pinned down. To remind him of that a dozen shots flew overhead, one neatly clipping a branch from a big pine. It thudded to the ground a few feet away.

Ruff began to move. There wasn't much hope of getting back off the hill, nor could he remain where he was. Sooner or later the searching bullets would find him.

He got into a crouch and began running uphill, weaving through the trees until he reached a narrow gulley and flung himself into it, moving again as soon as he touched bottom. Upslope again, the air in the gulley close and menacing, the day momentarily deceptively silent.

The Sioux popped up from behind a rock like one of those tin bears in a shooting gallery, and Ruff Justice fired the .56 from his hip. The bullet tore most of the Indian's head away, and he cartwheeled back soundlessly. There hadn't been time to scream. Ruff crouched and waited. Sweat trickled down his throat, dripped annoyingly into his eyes. He gave it a full minute and then went on.

The gulley petered out and he was up and into timber and rock again. Looking down through the trees, he could see Hart, indecisive, still out of range.

The bullet whined off the rocks beside Justice and he scurried behind them to halt, panting, the Spencer cool in his hand, comforting. To wait, to watch, knowing that Stone Hand wasn't the kind to pull off, to leave Justice alive. The man lived to kill. Every living man was regarded as an enemy. He would come.

Ruff saw the flash of color, heard the simultaneous drumming of hoofs. Whirling around, his back to the big gray boulder, he saw the mounted Sioux charging downslope, feathers flying, mouth open in a war cry.

Ruff felt the Indian's bullet hit the rock behind him and go singing off, felt the stone chips fly against his hand and face. The .56 spoke again and the big bay the Indian rode went down, a bullet through its heart. The horse rolled and the Indian, a look of astonishment on his face, went down, the horse crushing him as it landed.

There were more shots from upslope and Ruff took to his heels, moving through the timber, still weaving his way up the hill.

He crept up toward a rocky ridge. The serrated edge of the stony rise was shaped like a comb, whetted and polished by the winds of eons. From there Ruff could see the Red River of the North winding its way through the trees, glinting silver and deep blue.

For half an hour, as the sun began its slow descent, he stayed motionless, watching, listening, the sweat cooling his body. Then he heard it—a horse whickering in the pines farther along the ridge. Stone Hand had not pulled out. He knew the soldiers could not get to him, knew he had only one man to contend with—Ruff Justice—and by now he knew Ruff Justice had teeth.

Ruff moved uphill again, his feet whispering against the pine needle-carpeted earth. He saw a flash of color, then made out the paint pony standing regarding him with curiosity, ears pricked, eyes alert. A second horse—one with Paley's brand—stood across the clearing, head bowed, nibbling at the poor forage.

There was no one around, and then there was. The knife striking at his throat was the first thing Ruff saw, long before his senses registered the bronzed hand which held it, the muscular body behind it. Justice jerked back, striking upward and out with the heavy muzzle of his Spencer. It hit hard, tearing the jawbone of the Sioux before him. Blood rushed from the Indian's throat and he pawed at his face his eyes wild, dark, and savage.

He was on the ground, writhing, when Justice finished the job with his bowie.

He never heard the approaching footsteps, saw no shadow against the ground. Stone Hand's body collided with Ruff's, and his ax fell as Justice jerked his head away, striking back with fists and knees as the two men tumbled to the earth together, rolling downslope, Ruff's bowie lying where it had landed.

Stone Hand was massive and powerful. Quick and deadly. Ruff had his ax hand at the wrist, his leg hooked around the back of the Sioux warrior's knee.

They rolled down the slope, locked together in violent combat, then went off the lip of the stony shelf and dropped thirty feet to the ground below. Their faces were so near that Ruff could feel the Indian's hot breath against his cheek, see the crazed eyes, hear the grunt of effort as Stone Hand fought to tear his ax from Ruff's grip.

They hit the ground hard and Justice felt the wind

rush out of his body. He rolled away—too slowly—
and got to his feet in a defensive crouch. It wasn't
necessary. None of it was. Stone Hand lay against
the earth unmoving, his leg crooked under him.

Walking to him, Ruff first kicked the ax away
from the limp hand of the Sioux, then crouched to
examine the man. Alive. Bleeding from a head wound.
Stone Hand had landed against a saddle-sized rock,
his head cracking against it. He lay unconscious, his
savagely scarred face nearly peaceful.

Justice bent down, hefted the man, and throwing
him across his shoulder, started downslope toward
the flats.

Hart was still holding back when Ruff emerged
from the timber, but at the sight of Justice and his
burden, the cavalry came forward, closing the distance
rapidly. They found Ruff Justice sitting on the inert
form of Stone Hand, arms dangling between his
legs, cold blue eyes curiously expressionless.

"Is that . . . ?"

"It's him. I got four of them, including Stone
Hand. That should be all. You might want to comb
the hill, though. I could use my horse. Left a gun, a
knife, and a good Stetson up there too, if anyone
cares to look."

Hart took the suggestion. The cavalrymen clustered
around Stone Hand, watching as Hart put manacles
on the still-unconscious man. A lot of suggestions
were made about extralegal punishment.

"Skin him. Just nail him to that tree and skin him.
If they hang him it's not good enough."

"If you ask me . . ."

Ruff didn't ask. He was leaning against the saddle
of his recovered gray horse, watching sundown stain
the skies orange and deep crimson above the piney
ridge. He ached. His shoulder with the old wounds

especially. And his ribcage on the right side, his hip, left arm. He had a dull, constant headache.

"Ready?" Hart rested a hand on Ruff's shoulder, a gesture Justice didn't care for much. Hart was new at Fort Lincoln, however, new in the West—he didn't know the land or its men. He was tall, fair, competent when it came to book work, constantly muddled in the field.

"I'm ready."

"You'll get special mention in my report," Hart promised.

"Thanks." Ruff had had special mention—of various kinds—in many reports. It had never gotten him anything tangible. He tightened the cinches to his Texas-rigged saddle and swung up on the gray, which seemed surprised.

When Hart was ready, they filed out through the dusky light toward Fort Abraham Lincoln. Stone Hand was tied onto his horse's back, swaying and lurching. He came suddenly alert in the twilight, and his blood-scabbed face set as he saw what had happened. He tried to tear himself free, but his manacles had been lashed securely to the pommel of the saddle, his feet tied together beneath the horse's belly. He went nowhere and he sat glaring, muttering in his own tongue until he caught sight of Ruff Justice riding beside him.

"You," he said, and his voice was a growl, scarcely human, deep and quite mad, "I will kill. I will kill you if I have to crawl out of my grave to do it!"

Ruff burped politely and guided his gray away from the column. He wasn't in the mood.

Fort Lincoln had been quiet when they rode in through the main gate, the only signs of activity the lights in the enlisted barracks and the BOQ, a few men standing in front of the sutler's store drinking beer. Within minutes that all changed as word spread that Stone Hand had been brought in.

Men rushed out of the barracks; lamps were lighted everywhere. Somehow word had spread to the nearby town of Bismarck already, and in spring buggies and on horseback people were racing toward the fort.

Ruff had never cared for a circus, not even Bill Cody's variety. He unsaddled, rubbed his horse down, saw to it that the gray was well-grained, and headed back toward his quarters, seeing the gathering mob across the parade ground.

He shaved slowly with his ebony-handled razor, patting his face dry, washed up in the basin, then stretched out on his bunk, shirtless despite the chill of the evening.

"Mr. Justice?" The voice sounded before the knock on his door, and Justice rolled his head to glare at Corporal Willard Trask.

"Yes," he said wearily.

"Colonel MacEnroe would like to see you—his quarters."

Ruff just stared for a moment. If MacEnroe wanted to slap him on the back or shake his hand, he wanted no part of it. Nor did he want to write a report.

"What is it? Stone Hand?"

"No, sir. I don't think so. Something else has come up."

"All right. Five minutes."

Trask, grinning at some private joke, went out, and Ruff sat up with a small groan, reaching for his shirt. Dressing slowly, he brushed his long dark hair, smoothed his mustache down, strapped on his gun belt, and went out. Across parade something was still going on. The guardhouse was ringed by spectators, the sort of spectators who turn into lynch mobs; but MacEnroe had a dozen armed guards standing stone-faced around the place, and Ruff knew that the colonel, now that the townspeople had had their look, wouldn't be long in running them off the post.

Ruff strode across the parade ground, achieved the boardwalk, and made his way toward the commanding officer's quarters. Passing the orderly room, he found Fort Lincoln's vastly overweight, amiable first sergeant standing in the doorway, watching the activity across the way.

"Hello, Ruff."

"Mack." Justice nodded to Mack Pierce. "Going to run them off soon?"

"Yes." Mack spat. "Although if it were up to me, I'd as soon let them have him. Tear him apart, they would."

"Vicious tonight, aren't you?"

Pierce laughed. "It's age comin' on me. Still, Stone Hand's no good to anyone. He killed his own wife, you know? Battered one of his kids until the boy's crippled."

"I didn't know that."

"You don't know Bear Foot?" Mack asked with some surprise.

"Bear Foot, sure." He was a well-known hanger-on at the fort. A kid of fifteen or sixteen who hung around the paddock all day, liked to watch the soldiers drill, and who, although thrown out every evening at taps, returned right on time for reveille the next day. "I just didn't know he was anything to Stone Hand."

"Yep. His kid. The colonel's banned him from the post now. Had to. Could be he'd still do something for his father; could be he'd cut his throat, too—either way it can't be allowed."

"What's the colonel want me for now, Mac?"

"That"—Pierce smiled—"now that's a surprise, Ruff. You'll find out."

Justice scowled, nodded a good-night, and walked

along the plank walk to Colonel MacEnroe's quarters.

He rapped on the colonel's door and was summoned inside. MacEnroe sat with his boots propped up on a low, leather-covered hassock, his tunic partly unbuttoned, a glass of whiskey in his hand. It was unusual to see the colonel looking even partially at ease, but he did this evening.

"Sit down, Ruff. Good piece of work today."

"A lot of curiosity out there."

"I've had them all herded off for tonight. I suppose in the morning they'll be back. Stone Hand is a curiosity. He won't be for long," MacEnroe added soberly, finishing his drink. He stroked his silver mustache thoughtfully. "He's ranting over there. He wants the tall man in buckskins. Swears he'll kill you."

Ruff shrugged. You couldn't go around worrying about things like that. Besides, it didn't look as if Stone Hand was going to be killing anyone again.

"He'll be hanged day after tomorrow. What I called you over for," MacEnroe said, abruptly changing the subject, "was to find out if you mightn't be interested in doing something a little different."

Ruff's eyes narrowed. MacEnroe's ideas of something a little different had proven highly hazardous in the past.

"Such as?"

"Sit down, Ruff, for God's sake, and quit glaring at me like that; it's nothing like that Spirit Woman business; quite simple, really. But important—to me."

"All right. I'm always agreeable to suggestions you've got," Ruff said, and a flicker of amusement danced in his eyes. MacEnroe shook his head. Yes, Ruff took suggestions—sometimes. Ruff was a maverick, hardheaded, sometimes whimsical, sometimes just plain intractable. He was also the best rough country scout on the plains, and MacEnroe counted himself lucky to have him, past disagreements aside.

"A friend of mine will be arriving in the morning. Walter Court. We grew up together, separated during the war, met again at Fort Kearney—he was sutler there by that time, Now he's coming to Dakota." MacEnroe hesitated, "He's going to set up a freight line between here and Bear Creek."

"He is, is he?" Ruff said quietly. Justice was standing next to the fireplace, studying the twisting and turning of the gold and crimson flames.

"I know, I know. It's damn close to the Black Hills. Very bad territory, but that's what the man wants to do, and not being able to dissuade him, I promised to help. He's hoping for the mail contract, a little passenger trade, and miners' supplies."

"He doesn't know the country then, sir." Ruff turned slowly and fixed those icy blue eyes on MacEnroe. "There's the Sioux for starters, some of the roughtest up- and down-hill country in Dakota, every hijack artist on the plains sitting out there waiting to lift whatever gold they're digging out of Bear Creek now. You mentioned mail and freight— what about Anson Boggs? He's got the mail contract right now, doesn't he?"

"Yes, and you know how well he's handling it. Half of the stuff seems to be rifled before it reaches its destination. The postmaster hasn't got anything on Boggs, but he's damned unhappy with his work. And without the mail contract the freight won't pay its way—too damned far out. So it looks as if Boggs is on his way out."

"And he's supposed to stand still for it?" Ruff wagged his head. Boggs was big, ugly, no good, a drunk with three sons who were exact replicas of the old man down to their slovenly habits.

"It—uh—may be a little difficult at first." The colonel was fond of understatement.

"It may be. What is it you expect me to do, sir?"

"I'd like you to help him set up, that's all. Locate the three stations he's planning on using, trail blaze, guide him through the first weeks, Ruff. It would mean a lot to me. I owe this man. If I could I'd use my troopers, but you know I can't. You're next best."

Ruff had been mulling it over. There was hazard involved, but there was a hazard involved in whatever a man did in these times, in this area. Boggs had had first choice of sites for his way stations, but Justice thought he had chosen unwisely. There was no water half the time at Columbine Creek where he had his first station. Nor could he use Walker's Pass during bad weather. That could be improved upon, and if MacEnroe's friend was any kind of man he could easily improve the service Boggs was offering now.

"Why not," he said at length. "Beats going after Red Cloud."

"Which reminds me," MacEnroe said, and he was off again on an idea he had for doing just that, if Regiment would lend him another company. Ruff listened politely for half an hour, then headed off to bed.

When he walked to the colonel's office an hour after reveille, there were already numbers of people gathered around the stockade, hoping for a glimpse of Stone Hand. A few people, misinformed, had come and gone in disappointment. The hanging wasn't until tomorrow. That would be a big day, Ruff thought, wondering at the species.

There were half a dozen civilian mounts standing in front of the orderly room, a spring wagon, and two pack mules. Walter Court, Ruff decided, had arrived.

Mack Pierce, perspiring, harried, sat at his desk shuffling papers. The corporal of the guard sat in the corner, hands behind his head, looking at a fly on the ceiling.

"Court?" Ruff asked Pierce.

"Yes, dammit," Pierce muttered.

Ruff frowned. "Something the matter?"

"Isn't it?" Mack replied. "Go on in. There's a hell of a surprise waiting for you."

Exciting Westerns by Jon Sharpe from SIGNET

*Prices slightly higher in Canada

**Buy them at your local
bookstore or use coupon
on next page for ordering.**

Exciting Westerns by Jon Sharpe